"No matter what happens, Iron Soldier and I have to stay out front..."

Max stared at the three gunmen. "I took the lead out of Cheyenne and I don't want to be passed. Spike, you, Ed, and Jess are going to slow the Gunsmith down."

The three gunmen exchanged glances. Spike was their leader, a dark, taciturn man with a hard reputation. "You want us to stop him, or just slow him?"

"Slow him, I said! Don't kill him or his horse. It's too early for anything so drastic."

"Boss," Spike protested, "he's gonna keep coming unless he's dead! You know that as well as I do. Let us just put a bullet into him. We can take his body and shove his boot through his stirrup and let that horse drag him until there ain't nothing to recognize . . ."

Also in THE GUNSMITH series

- MACKLIN'S WOMEN
- THE CHINESE GUNMEN
- THE WOMAN HUNT
- THE GUNS OF ABILENE
- THREE GUNS FOR GLORY
- LEADTOWN
- THE LONGHORN WAR
- QUANAH'S REVENGE
- HEAVYWEIGHT GUN
- NEW ORLEANS FIRE
- ONE-HANDED GUN
- THE CANADIAN PAYROLL
- DRAW TO AN INSIDE DEATH
- DEAD MAN'S HAND
- BANDIT GOLD
- BUCKSKINS AND SIX-GUNS
- SILVER WAR
- HIGH NOON AT LANCASTER
- BANDIDO BLOOD
- THE DODGE CITY GANG
- SASQUATCH HUNT
- BULLETS AND BALLOTS
- THE RIVERBOAT GANG
- KILLER GRIZZLY
- NORTH OF THE BORDER
- EAGLE'S GAP
- CHINATOWN HELL
- THE PANHANDLE SEARCH
- WILDCAT ROUNDUP
- THE PONDEROSA WAR
- TROUBLE RIDES A FAST HORSE
- DYNAMITE JUSTICE
- THE POSSE
- NIGHT OF THE GILA
- THE BOUNTY WOMEN
- BLACK PEARL SALOON
- GUNDOWN IN PARADISE
- KING OF THE BORDER
- THE EL PASO SALT WAR
- THE TEN PINES KILLER
- HELL WITH A PISTOL
- THE WYOMING CATTLE KILL
- THE GOLDEN HORSEMAN
- THE SCARLET GUN
- NAVAHO DEVIL
- WILD BILL'S GHOST
- THE MINER'S SHOWDOWN
- ARCHER'S REVENGE
- SHOWDOWN IN RATON
- WHEN LEGENDS MEET
- DESERT HELL
- THE DIAMOND GUN
- DENVER DUO
- HELL ON WHEELS
- THE LEGEND MAKER
- WALKING DEAD MAN
- CROSSFIRE MOUNTAIN
- THE DEADLY HEALER
- THE TRAIL DRIVE WAR
- GERONIMO'S TRAIL
- THE COMSTOCK GOLD FRAUD
- BOOMTOWN KILLER
- TEXAS TRACKDOWN
- THE FAST DRAW LEAGUE
- SHOWDOWN IN RIO MALO
- OUTLAW TRAIL
- HOMESTEADER GUNS
- FIVE CARD DEATH
- TRAILDRIVE TO MONTANA
- TRIAL BY FIRE
- THE OLD WHISTLER GANG
- DAUGHTER OF GOLD
- APACHE GOLD
- PLAINS MURDER
- DEADLY MEMORIES
- THE NEVADA TIMBER WAR
- NEW MEXICO SHOWDOWN
- BARBED WIRE AND BULLETS
- DEATH EXPRESS
- WHEN LEGENDS DIE
- SIX-GUN JUSTICE
- MUSTANG HUNTERS
- TEXAS RANSOM
- VENGEANCE TOWN

WINNER TAKE ALL

J. R. ROBERTS

JOVE BOOKS, NEW YORK

THE GUNSMITH #85: WINNER TAKE ALL

A Jove book/published by arrangement with
the author

PRINTING HISTORY
Jove edition/January 1989

All rights reserved.
Copyright © 1989 by Robert J. Randisi.
This book may not be reproduced in whole or in part,
by mimeograph or any other means, without permission.
For information address: The Berkley Publishing Group,
200 Madison Avenue, New York, New York 10016.

ISBN: 0-515-09877-9

Jove books are published by The Berkley Publishing Group,
200 Madison Avenue, New York, New York 10016.
The name "JOVE" and the "J" logo
are trademarks belonging to Jove Publications, Inc.

PRINTED IN THE UNITED STATES OF AMERICA

10 9 8 7 6 5 4 3 2 1

ONE

Clint Adams rode into Cheyenne, Wyoming, on the Fourth of July and the town was exploding with more noise than a string of Chinese firecrackers. By noon, most of the cowboys were drunk, and those who were still sober were doing their goddamnedest to catch up with their friends. The Union Pacific Railroad had a special train in town, and it kept blasting its whistle and scaring the hell out of the horses. Out on the eastern limits of Cheyenne at least a thousand people were watching a wide-open rodeo with the meanest broncs that could be found doing their best to pitch and then stomp the best cowboys in the territory.

Clint rode through the streets of Cheyenne missing nothing. The town had mushroomed overnight when the transcontinental railroad had come bustling across southern Wyoming. But unlike many of the other tent cities that flowered and then withered with the passing of the construction crews, Cheyenne had survived and had even begun to grow. Mostly it was because the Union Pacific had designated it as one of its main stations, where trains were to be disconnected and repaired in huge, tin roundhouses. Cheyenne was first and last a railroad town, but its economy had expanded to include promising cattle ranches and even some timbering.

Cheyenne had one other big advantage, and that was the fact that it was the natural junction of another railroad that would soon be built up from Denver down to the south. But the Gunsmith wasn't thinking about all the reasons for the town's growth, instead, he was sizing up the opportunities to make a little money for himself. Clint had won just over a thousand dollars in Denver only the week before, but he liked to spend money on himself and his black gelding Duke, and he did not like to do things second-class. He wore nice clothes, stayed in good hotels, and ate well. Then, too, there were always little unexpected emergencies that a man needed to carry money for. Things like running into especially beautiful women who deserved to be wined and dined in high style and then taken on moonlit buggy rides. Those sorts of things.

As the Gunsmith rode through the celebrations, he did not see another gunsmith shop. He weighed the possibility of opening a shop of his own but discarded the idea. What he wanted was to enjoy himself with a little poker and then move along. The days were hot, and he was thinking it would be nice to find himself some cool mountains. In July, August, and September, a man who could afford to relax owed it to himself to smell the pines, swim in a cold mountain stream or lake, and then spend some time trout fishing.

Nope, Clint thought as he surveyed the busy saloons and saw how packed the streets were with cowboys determined to let off steam and raise hell, I guess I really don't want to work this summer. Maybe I could come back and gunsmith in the fall. But then, that was getting mighty close to winter, and Cheyene could be brutal with its arctic-spawned blizzards.

Clint allowed as how he'd just spend a day, maybe two, and pass on toward the Sierra Nevada Mountains. He had some business in Carson City, and Lake Tahoe was just a few miles up the mountainside. He had a yearning to visit that lake, and he was thinking he might just put Duke in a railroad stock car and travel in style across the searing deserts of Utah and Nevada. The Paiute Indians were supposed to be on the prod lately, and it seemed like the smart thing for a man with a thousand dollars to do.

"Hey!" someone yelled, "aren't you the Gunsmith?"

Clint turned to see a cowboy limping toward him. "Shorty Evans, is that you?"

"Hell yes, it is! Who'd you think it was, Napoleon Bone-a-part?"

Clint grinned. Shorty Evans was a bronc-buster who'd once helped him out down in Santa Fe, New Mexico, when some polecat had ambushed him and left him for dead. Shorty had come along and found him and saved his life. "You look good!" Clint said, though it was not entirely the truth. Shorty had always walked with a limp in his left leg, but now he moved as if his bones were connected by barbed wire and every movement was a-jabbin' him hard.

"Aw, the hell I do! I look and move like I was a hundred years old. Damn!" Shorty said, "Every time I see that black gelding you ride I just slobber all over myself. Is he still as fast as he was last time I saw him outrun that Santa Fe mare they said couldn't be beat?"

"He's frisky as ever," Clint said. "I might be slowing down, but he sure isn't."

"Ha! I bet you're still the fastest gun between San Francisco and St. Louis!"

Clint squirmed a little in his saddle as men stared at him with sudden interest. "Gunfighting is a little like taking a married woman to bed, Shorty. If you do it too often, no matter how good you are at sneaking out bedroom windows and climbing over backyard fences, sooner or later, it'll get you killed."

Shorty doubled up with laughter. "Jesus, Clint! You sure got a way with the words and the ladies. I've missed ya!"

"Then point us to the best saloon in town and we'll have a couple of drinks for old-time's sake."

Shorty nodded eagerly. "Why, sure," he said. "Damn right I—"

"*Won't*," a tall, thin man riding a big dapple horse said, cutting between them. "Or are you quitting your job?"

Clint turned in his saddle, and his first impression of the intruder was not favorable. The man's expression was angry and arrogant. He rode a little English-type saddle and held a whip in his leather riding gloves. His face was hawkishly handsome and his nose was aquiline. He had dark brown hair and hard, black eyes, though the dapple-gray stallion he was riding was one of the finest-looking animals that Clint had ever seen. It was as tall as Duke, just over sixteen hands and a little finer-boned. The dapple danced nervously, and anyone who looked at it knew there was plenty of that rich Eastern racing blood in its veins. At least half thoroughbred, maybe three-quarters, it was built to run.

"Mr. Holloway!" Shorty stammered, clearly unnerved by the prospect of losing his job. "I was only kidding about that drink. I was just on my way out to the racetrack right this second."

"You damn sure better have been. You know I got a thousand dollars of my own money riding on a race that's to start in less than fifteen minutes. And you're supposed to be my handler! What in the hell good are you for anything else?"

"Now wait just a minute," Clint said. "That's no way to speak to one of the finest bronc-busters that ever—"

"Was is right," the man hissed. "He's a has-been who would have starved in the street last winter if I hadn't given him a job. And right now, his job is to help me win the next race on Iron Soldier."

Clint blinked. "That's Iron Soldier? Why, I heard of him all the way down to Texas. He's supposed to be one of the finest racing horses in the country."

Holloway relaxed at the compliment. "He is. Fastest horse in the West. I own and train him. Shorty, when he's sober, assists me."

Shorty blushed with humiliation. "I've trained some good running horses in my day, Mr. Holloway. I did more than just bust broncs. And I'll tell you something, right now I'm standing before the two fastest horses I ever laid eyes on."

Holloway's eyes narrowed. He studied Duke with sudden interest. "Is he really that fast?"

Clint never bragged. "He can run a little. But—"

"Aw," Shorty said. "Don't be so damned modest, Clint. Why, you won almost three thousand dollars just in Santa Fe on Duke. Won over that mare by a good two lengths, and she was supposed to be the fastest thing in the whole damned territory."

"Perhaps you'd like to race Iron Soldier," Holloway said, "after he finishes his race and has an hour or two to rest up."

"No, thanks," Clint said. "We've been doing some hard riding the past few days, I'm just looking for a place to board him and then to lay my head."

"Nonsense! It's the Fourth of July. Let's give the people of Cheyenne a real race!"

"Not interested," Clint said again. "Besides, it isn't right that a horse like that should have to run twice in the same day."

"Then race me tomorrow. I'll give you odds."

"Nope."

Holloway frowned. "Maybe Shorty was just bragging when he said your gelding could run. Seems to me like he was probably just shooting off his mouth, as usual."

Clint's face hardened. He did not like to be baited, and he liked even less having Shorty insulted. "What kind of odds will you give me?"

"Two to one, same as everyone else."

Shorty stepped back and held up all his fingers so that Holloway could not see him.

"I heard you're more likely to give ten-to-one odds," Clint said.

"Not against that kind of horseflesh, I don't," Holloway growled. "Besides, you and that horse are pretty famous yourselves. Be a shame if everyone in Cheyenne learned you was chicken to race."

"Mister," Clint said, a hard edge creeping into his voice, "if you call me 'chicken' again, I'll ram my fist down your gullet and yank you plumb inside out."

Holloway stiffened. "You may be famed for your gunfighting, but I'm famed for my long-distance riding. I was a Pony Express rider a few years ago and I learned the meaning of hardship and rising to meet the test. I won't fight you, but if you care to put your horse up against mine, then you be out there at the track in about two hours. Otherwise, the word will go out that you declined to race. I'll let the people of Cheyenne make up their own minds about the reason. Shorty, you come along!"

"Yes, sir!"

Clint said nothing as Holloway touched Iron Soldier with spurs and galloped out of town.

"You'd stand a fair chance of beating 'em," Shorty called, as he hurried away. "That is, if Duke ain't lost any speed. Think about it!"

"I already did," Clint said angrily as he reined his horse

and proceeded down the street toward Belcher's Livery.

He had paid the liveryman and was unsaddling Duke and getting ready to put him in a stall when a soft female voice said, "So, you're the Gunsmith, and this is Duke. I've heard a lot about you both from Shorty."

Clint's hands fell away from his cinch when he looked up and saw the woman who had spoken. She was petite, only about five feet two, but every inch of it was perfect. She wore a burgundy-colored dress of lace and chiffon and a pretty hat with a wide brim and plumed white feathers. She had black hair, long black lashes, and green eyes. Her skin was as flawless as that of a porcelain doll and her full lips were pursed in interest and faint amusement. She had an hour-glass figure and her perfume was French, very expensive.

"And who might you be?" he asked. "Max Holloway's personal emmisary?"

She surprised him by laughing. "In a way, yes!" she said. "How did you guess?"

"Well," Clint said. "Ladies of the night or dance-hall girls can't afford those clothes or that perfume. Neither can school marms. Church-going women wouldn't be caught in here alone with a stranger. You just don't fit any of the molds, so I took a wild guess. You have to be Holloway's woman."

"I'm my *own* woman," she said, the laughter in her voice dying.

"Then why are you here?"

She moved closer to the horse, her eyes studying him with evident approval. "He's big and strong, yet built for running. Is he a thoroughbred?"

"Nope, though I suspect there's some of that breeding lurking in his background somewhere."

"He's as tall as Iron Soldier. How old is he?"

"About seven."

"That's perfect," she said. "Right in his prime. Some people like to run three-year olds, but they can't stand up to the heavy track we have out here. Iron Soldier could run five miles through sand and not break a sweat. Max keeps him in top running condition. But your horse looks more than fit himself."

"He is that," Clint said. "But I told Holloway and I'll tell you the same. I'm not interested in a horse race."

She did not seem to be listening. "I have to warn you, you couldn't get the usual ten-to-one odds. Max has already asked around and there are a few men here in town who've seen your horse run. They say he's as fast as the Iron Soldier. Max wouldn't give you more than three-to-one odds."

"Three-to-one is good odds. I usually give them rather than get them. But no, I still—"

"Please race the man!"

Clint had been about to pull the saddle off Duke but the tone of her voice stopped him cold. "Why is it so important to you?"

She touched his arm. Her face was close. "Max Holloway is conceited, boorish, and absolutely insufferable. He's never been beaten . . . at least not for years. A defeat would be the best thing in the world for him. Maybe it would even make him a little more tolerant of weakness . . . even failure. I know this much, it would make him a lot more human."

"I'm sorry," Clint said. "But Max Holloway's disposition is of no concern to me one way or the other."

Her shoulders sagged. "I see. I'd hoped that . . . never mind."

She started to turn away but he caught her by the elbow and gently turned her around. "What did you hope?"

"That my welfare might interest you, Mr. Adams."

Her lips seemed to glisten and her perfume was like a

love potion. She was stunning.

"A beautiful woman's welfare always concerns me, Mrs. Holloway."

"Miss Flowers," she corrected. "My name is Victoria Flowers."

She stood up on her toes and closed her eyes. When their lips met, Clint crushed her in his arms, and if she hadn't have been so nicely dressed, he'd have scooped her up and carried her to the hayloft.

She pulled away breathlessly. "If you race Iron Soldier today, I'll make you glad."

"Win or lose?" Clint was fully aware that Iron Soldier had never been beat. Duke was a remarkable running horse, but sooner or later, every gunslinger and every horse got beat by another that was a shade faster.

"Win . . . or lose," she whispered. "I promise."

Clint swallowed. He could feel the crotch of his pants getting tighter and tighter. "Then I'll do it," he said thickly.

She touched his cheek, tracing a faint scar. "You won't be sorry."

Clint tightened his cinch. As long as this woman kept her promise, he knew full well he wouldn't be sorry, even if he lost all his money.

TWO

Clint waited almost an hour to rest and lightly grain Duke before he rode back out onto the main street and angled Duke toward the racetrack. The moment he emerged from the livery, a huge and noisy throng of men cheered and fell into his wake. Their presence irritated the Gunsmith just a shade because it seemed obvious that everyone in Cheyenne knew that Miss Victoria Flowers had gone alone into the livery to change his mind and make a horse race. And it also seemed plenty obvious that no one was surprised Miss Flowers had somehow managed to change the Gunsmith's mind. In fact, he heard a few ribald remarks along those lines.

But in truth, Clint was already beginning to feel his blood quicken over the upcoming match. He knew that the Iron Soldier had raced on the East Coast for several years before "retiring" from the track, only to vanish and reappear out West. Max Holloway had paid a small fortune for the animal which had been starting to slip just a little and would eventually have met his match in Sarotoga or some other famed eastern racing town. But out in the West, the competition was not nearly so stiff. Oh, there were some very fast horses, but not many were bred for the track or had much thoroughbred blood. So the Iron Soldier had found the pickings to his liking and, if he'd lost a couple of seconds over a mile track, it wasn't noticed, because he still had blazing speed.

This impression was not changed when Clint learned that Iron Soldier had beaten his opponent, a flashy roan mare said to be the fastest horse in Montana, by only a neck. Most likely, the gray stallion could have won by several lengths but Max Holloway had held him in to make the race look competitive. Max was too smart to allow his horse to win by much no matter how superior the gray stallion might be. Easy wins might feel good, but they drove up the odds and scared off future competition. No, the way to win a horse race—and to keep winning horse races—was to make it appear as if your horse was sure to be defeated next time. Always, next time.

Shorty was grinning from ear to ear when he rode up to the track and dismounted. "I told Mr. Holloway you'd run," he crowed. "I know you, Clint. You're too much of a gambler to walk away from two-to-one odds."

"Two-to-one! I was told it would be three-to-one."

"Against Duke!" Shorty wagged his head. "Hell, man. Be reasonable. That ain't no crow-bait Indian pony you're riding."

"I know that," Clint groused. "But next time, I'd appreciate it if you'd stop going around telling everyone how fast my horse is. It serves no good purpose and it'll cut into my winnings."

"Ha! So you really do expect to win!"

"Of course I do. How much do I need to bet?"

"A thousand would be fine."

Clint frowned. If he lost, he'd be down to his last few dollars. But if he won, he'd have three thousand dollars and that was more money than he'd had at one time in longer than he cared to remember.

"All right," he said. "Who's holding the money?"

"Mr. Dave Cutter, the man over there with the tall white Stetson."

"Is he honest?" Clint had been cheated before and he wanted no more of it.

"As the day is long . . . come December."

Clint frowned and rode Duke through the crowd toward Mr. Cutter. People were shoving and trying to get a better look at Duke. Most were saying that he was a mighty fine-looking horse, but too heavily muscled to run fast. Clint tuned out the idle talk and when he reached Cutter, he said, "I understand the odds are three-to-one against me."

"Two-to-one," Cutter said. "Your friend has been telling everyone about that race down in Santa Fe. Shorty isn't much good anymore, but there's no one around who'd deny he knows a fast horse when he sees one run. And he says that black gelding of yours can fly."

"So can his mouth," Clint said, as he pulled out his roll of money. "I'll put a thousand dollars down at two-to-one. I guess I don't have to tell you what I'm inclined to do with someone who cheats me."

Cutter's thin smile slipped badly. "No," he said, taking Clint's money. "You sure don't. Your reputation leaves little to the imagination."

"Good," Clint said. "Just as long as we understand each other. Tell me where and how far we race."

"Five miles. Out to that lone pine tree way out yonder on that low bluff and then come on back. Finish line is right where we are now."

Clint was stunned. "I thought this was supposed to be on the racetrack!"

"Nope. Last one was, but not this one."

Clint swore in anger. He could barely see the tree and the ground looked damned rough to run full tilt across. There were at least two dry riverbeds to cross and a stretch of rocky ground. No telling how many prairie-dog holes they'd have to worry about. "I don't like it," he said.

"I'm sorry to hear that, Gunsmith."

Clint looked over to see Max Holloway riding Iron Soldier and grinning with satisfaction. "But now that you've laid down your bet . . . well, I'm afraid you either have to run or forfeit your thousand dollars. Couldn't blame you for doing that. You see, I know every foot of ground across that stretch to the tree and back, but you sure don't. If you want to avoid your horse stepping into a hole, you'll have to follow me. Isn't that right, Vicki?"

Clint glanced over and saw Miss Victoria Flowers. Vicki, she was called. The young beauty smiled apologetically. When Holloway turned his back on her for an instant, she gave Clint a seductive wink that promised everything short of heaven.

"Let's get this thing started," Clint said. "That is, if your stallion has recovered."

"That last race just warmed him up," Holloway said. "Cutter, relieve Mr. Adams of his weapons and then have someone mark us a starting and finishing line."

Clint's hand touched the butt of his six-gun. "You can take my saddle rifle, but not my six-gun."

"But . . . but Mr. Holloway has handed over his arms."

"Then give them back to him if he wants. I keep my gun."

Holloway was not pleased. "In that case, I believe I will take my pistol back," he said.

Cutter handed him his six-gun and holster. Clint would have bet anything that the man was also wearing a hideout derringer and a knife. It would have been sheer madness to have disarmed himself and been at Holloway's mercy. Men had been shot for a lot less money than that being wagered on this race.

The crowd parted and gave them plenty of starting room.

Someone had, of all things, a Civil War saber and it was used to cut a line in the dirt for them to cross.

"Any rules?" Clint asked, feeling Duke start to tense as the big horse understood what was about to happen. Duke laid his ears back as the stallion pawed the ground and then tried to bite and kick. Clint was angry. "Control your horse, dammit!"

Holloway pulled his hat down tight over his forehead. He was taller than Clint but slender and his saddle was lighter. Iron Soldier was carrying about forty pounds less weight. The last bets were made.

"Frontier Rules. Anything goes."

Clint knew what that meant. It meant that it was to be a no-holds-barred race where the best man and the best horse were not only the fastest, but also the most ruthless. Given the distance, neither horse could be expected to run full out, so the race would go neck and neck until the homestretch. With two horses like Duke and Iron Soldier, the crowd could expect plenty of extra activity.

"On your mark, get set—" At least fifty guns exploded as the starter's shot was drowned by the crowd's firepower. Iron Soldier flew off the starting as if he'd been shot out of a cannon. He took an early lead, and Clint had to curb Duke hard in order to keep the black from challenging for the front.

"Just take it easy," he said, leaning forward in his saddle and talking to the horse. "Five miles is longer than we've ever raced before. Let's let the arrogant Max Holloway blaze a path to the tree. We'll overtake him on the way back."

Holloway saw at once that Clint was an experienced racer and was too smart to go rushing ahead. Iron Soldier was running as smooth and easy as a Swiss timepiece. The horse seemed to glide over the prairie. Clint let Duke stay right on his tail as the ground slid underneath their thundering hooves.

There were thousands of prairie-dog holes and some made by badgers, too. The badger holes were especially treacherous. They were about four inches wide and dropped straight down for better than three feet. If a running horse stepped in a badger hole, it was sure to bust its leg and somersault onto its rider.

They charged up the low rise of ground, and Iron Soldier whipped neatly around the tree as if he were a schoolboy playing touch-tag. It was damned obvious that the Cheyenne horse and rider had practiced that sharp reverse turn until they had it down perfectly. On the other hand, Clint and Duke went wide and lost far too much ground. By the time Clint and Duke were headed back toward the crowd, Iron Soldier had a good twenty-yard lead, and he was running full out with his ears pinned down.

Clint knew he had made a bad mistake, one he'd not foreseen. There was nothing to do but ask Duke to close ground and that's exactly what he did. The black gelding's eyes gleamed with fire and he stretched low to the earth and raced like the witches of hell were on his heels. Clint had to hang onto his hat as they blistered the trail, and to his and everyone else's amazement, he began to close in on the gray stallion.

Max Holloway twisted around in his special racing saddle and he could not believe his eyes as Duke came thundering up behind. He used his quirt and slashed Duke across his tender nose and the gelding threw his head back and momentarily lost stride.

Clint was furious! What he wanted to do was to pull his gun and pistol-whip the man in front of him but instead, he swerved Duke out and took his chances with the prairie-dog holes. The black gelding recovered his stride and again challenged Iron Soldier. Ten feet apart now, Duke inched up until they were running dead even.

The gray stallion had never been overtaken and he showed his character and heart by trying even harder. Over the next mile, he pulled away slightly until he was almost a full length ahead, then Clint shaved a few strides off their path and they were racing head-to-head again.

The wind was a roar in Clint's ears. Tears streamed from the corners of his eyes and he rode low in the saddle, bent forward, trying everything he could to make Duke's stride even smoother and more effortless. Max Holloway was doing the same. He was a superb rider and one that seemed to be part of the animal he rode.

Clint could now hear the shouts of the crowd up ahead. He raised his eyes and saw that there was less than a mile to go. "Come on, boy!" he yelled, "show them your heels!"

Duke threw himself forward, running like a thing possessed. He started to pull ahead and would have if Holloway hadn't quirted him across the eyes. Duke threw his head up and started to veer away. Clint was insane with anger. He lashed out with his boot and his spur caught the Holloway's stirrup just as Iron Soldier started to pull ahead.

Holloway shouted in alarm and the two horses were thrown off-stride and both lost their rhythm. Holloway cursed and lashed out again, only this time Clint leaned far forward and grabbed the quirt. He twisted it around his hand and yanked with all his might.

Max Holloway was torn from his horse. The little racing saddle had no saddlehorn to grab and he went crashing to the earth. He hit dirt and rolled over and over to lay still as Clint and Duke followed the riderless and now ineligible Iron Soldier across the finish line.

The crowd went insane. There was so much excitement

and confusion that Clint had a difficult time reaching Cutter. But when he did, he stuck out his hand and yelled, "All right, I won. Give me back my rifle and the purse!"

"But . . . but you cheated!"

"It was Frontier Rules! Holloway's rules. Pay me, damn you!"

Cutter gave him both his weapon and the money. All of it. But he was furious. "Iron Soldier crossed the finish line ahead of you. He won the race, not your horse."

"It's the rider, not the horse," Clint snapped. "Anyone knows that a riderless horse is disqualified from the race."

"You'll have to convince Mr. Holloway of that," Cutter shouted. "He won't buy this and neither will most of this crowd."

Clint helped catch the gray stallion and then he trotted back out to Holloway, who was dazed and badly bruised, but otherwise fine. His head was resting in Vicki Flower's lap. "Miss Flowers, can I give you a ride back to town?"

She looked up and shook her head. She looked very worried. Clint saw the way of things and decided that it would not be very gentlemanly to remind her of her veiled promise. Not here and not now. So he rode off alone, with Shorty being the only man to congratulate him.

Clint took no satisfaction in the race. It had been rigged and it had been dirty. But the better horse had won and he was two thousand dollars richer. All things considered, even though Miss Flowers had gone back on her promise, it had still been a very profitable day.

THREE

Clint finished his steak dinner and leaned back in his chair, content with the plush surroundings of the Antelope Bar & Grill. But as he prepared to order an after-dinner brandy, he looked up and saw Shorty hobbling across the dining room. Shorty's face was flushed from drinking and he appeared both out of place and out of sorts in the fancy restaurant. He looked to the left and the right as he marched to Clint's table with a waiter in tow.

"It's all right," Clint said impatiently. "He's my guest. Bring him whatever he wants to eat."

Shorty pulled up a chair. "Just bring me a bottle of something to drink. Something strong."

The waiter looked to Clint, who nodded, deciding that imported brandy would not be appreciated by the ex-broncbuster. "Whiskey, two glasses." When the man was gone, Clint said, "What's wrong?"

"I got fired."

"Why?"

Shorty shrugged his thin shoulders. "I guess because Holloway figures I warned you about that fast turn that Iron Soldier would have."

"You should have warned me."

"Yeah, I know. I know. But hell, you did good anyway.

Holloway usually gains such a big lead after that turn that he could walk Iron Soldier to the finish line and still win.''

"I'd still have done better if you'd have warned me," Clint said, not quite ready to forgive the man. "As it was, Duke had a lot of ground to make up."

"I know, but he did it! I bet on him. Five dollars. I think someone told Holloway I bet against him and that really finished things off."

"The man isn't worth worrying about," Clint said, as their whiskey and glasses were placed before them. The Gunsmith poured two full water glasses and they raised them in toast.

"To better times," Shorty said. "To a man's youth, when he can ride rough horses and rougher women."

Clint smiled at that, but a smile could not hide his concern. "What are you going to do now?" he asked gently.

"I don't know," Shorty admitted. "I'm too damned old and stoved-up to work off a horse and I can't stay on my feet too long. I just wish someone would pay wages for a chair rocker. That's about all I'm good for anymore."

Clint drank quickly. He remembered Shorty ten years ago, when he was still the pride of Santa Fe broncbusters. He'd been a natural horseman and a gifted rider. One of the best Clint had ever seen. "I'd like to help you," he said, reaching for his prize money.

"No!" Shorty lowered his voice as the other diners looked at them. "I won't take charity."

"All right, then it's a loan. Until you can pay me back."

Shorty shook his head. "You know I can't ever pay you back. I'm done. I been trying to get me a job as a hotel clerk, but everyone in town has seen me drunk a few times, and . . ."

Clint understood. He understood but he had no idea of what to say or do. When Shorty stood up to leave, Clint said, "Take the bottle. And here, take this money. If you try to give it back, I'll drag out my famous six-gun and put a hole through you and end your misery for keeps."

Shorty grinned. "Hell, you're as gentle as an old pussycat unless someone steps on your tail. How much is this?"

"Enough to buy you a rocking chair and a long vacation."

Shorty stared at the huge roll of greenbacks, and his voice was strained when he said, "It's all your winnings, ain't it?"

Clint didn't answer. But it was true. "It'd have been twice as much if you hadn't shot your flap about how fast Duke is. You cost us both."

"Yeah, but Jesus, ain't your Duke a piece of horse, though! I never seen the likes of him. Best animal I ever saw. Whatever fool gelded him ought to be castrated hisself. You could live off his stud fees."

"What's done is done," Clint said. The subject was one he did not care to discuss. It was a shame that Duke was a gelding. A damn waste.

"Clint, I got to ask you something."

"Then ask."

"If . . . if you hadn't ripped Holloway off his saddle, how bad do you think Duke would have beat Iron Soldier?"

"Couple of lengths is all," Clint said.

Shorty liked to hear that. "I believe you would have." He titled the bottle up toward the chandelier. After he drank a quarter of the bottle, he closed his eyes and sighed with contentment, oblivious of the disapproval of the waiter and the other diners. "You know, you're a hell of a friend, Clint. The best. And I got to give you another warning. Holloway is crying foul. He wants another race. A bigger one."

"He can race himself straight to hell," Clint said. "I won't do it again. We won and that is that."

"Not for Max Holloway. He'll find a way to force you

WINNER TAKE ALL 21

into a race. His pride won't stand up to losin'."

"His pride is *his* problem, not mine. So long, old-timer. You take care of yourself. I think I'll be leaving real early."

"Good idea," Shorty said. "Just bolt your door and keep your gun handy."

"Don't flash all that money around," Clint warned. "Put it in the bank and make it last awhile."

"I'll do that," the man said, as he hobbled away.

Clint waited a few minutes and then he paid his bill and headed for the door. As he was leaving, he was handed a note by his waiter. Out in the lobby, he opened it and read: MEET ME AT THE TRANSCONTINENTAL HOTEL LOBBY AT MIDNIGHT. V.F.

The Gunsmith frowned. V.F. had to mean Victoria Flowers. But why did she want to meet him? She'd made her loyalties plain enough for anyone to see. And even if she did want to talk, why at midnight?

It might well be a trap. Clint was always suspicious of midnight meetings, especially with beautiful strangers tied to the opposition. But on the other hand, they were usually interesting and sometimes highly entertaining. I'll hide my thousand dollars and go meet her, he thought. If I don't, I'll always wonder what would have happened.

He spent the evening in a couple of the less-rowdy saloons, playing poker without enthusiasm, his mind on Vicki. Clint was constantly interrupted by men who came up to congratulate him on the race. More than a few warned him that he had not heard the last of Max Holloway. To all of them, Clint just nodded his head and kept his mouth shut. In a day or two, he and Duke would be riding the Union Pacific out of Cheyenne and that would be the end of all this unpleasantness.

Once, he saw Shorty. Shorty was drinking, but not drunk,

and when he recognized the Gunsmith, he raised his glass in salute and winked like a conspirator. That relieved Clint, because he had been afraid the old man would get drunk and either gamble his money away, or get rolled and maybe killed in some dark alley. Maybe Shorty wasn't quite as far gone as he appeared. At least he was showing good sense.

At a quarter to twelve, Clint threw in his hand, having lost about thirty dollars. He didn't care. Maybe he'd come back tomorrow night with his mind more on the game and win tonight's losses back ten times over. With a little luck and a lot more concentration, Clint was sure that he could leave Cheyenne a winner at cards.

The Transcontinental Hotel was for women only and it was both fancy and respectable. No men were allowed upstairs and its foyer was well lit even at this hour. A very old desk clerk wore a tie and smiled to reveal his contracted gumline. There were spittoons on the floor for male visitors and the ubiquitous paintings of nymphs and naked ladies were absent from the walls. Instead, depictions of the transcontinental railroad adorned the walls. They were mostly lithographs, good ones that had been ordered from some Eastern catalogue store and even framed with wood and glass. One of them was a real oil painting, a scene reminiscent of the famed joining of the two railroads at Promontory, Utah. It was a famous subject for Western artists, and Clint started to walk over and admire the work when Vicki Flowers descended the stairway from the second floor. One look at her and Clint completely forgot about Promontory.

She was dressed in a silk gown that clung to her like skin on a banana. Every curve was accentuated and moving. Even the old hotel clerk, who must have been in his eighties, grinned toothlessly and licked his lips.

"Thank you for coming to see me," she purred.

"Who in his right mind wouldn't?"

WINNER TAKE ALL

She led Clint over to a high-backed sofa where they could not be seen or overheard by the clerk, who sat down behind his counter and fought to stay awake. "I wanted to explain about this afternoon," she began.

"What's there to explain?"

"Well, I . . . I did allude to certain . . . I sort of led you to believe. . . ."

She was having trouble so Clint decided to have mercy. "You led me to believe I'd be rewarded—win or lose—if I raced Max Holloway."

"Yes." She smiled sweetly. "I know I did. But I didn't say how I'd reward you."

"It didn't take much imagination to figure that one out," Clint said.

Her cheeks blushed red. "No, I guess it didn't. But when I saw Max, I thought he'd broken his neck or something, and I realized that I didn't hate him completely. Or maybe I realized that I had once loved and been married to him."

Clint blinked with surprise. "You were married to the man?"

"Why do you seem so surprised?"

"You just don't seem to match up. That's meant as a compliment."

"Thank you. But Max wasn't always so . . . ruthless. When we were married he was struggling. He inherited his uncle's cattle ranch just south of town and beef prices were terrible. Most ranchers tried to weather the storm and they went bankrupt. But Max thought differently. He bought Iron Soldier and began to race and breed him. He did very well. Other investments also paid off handsomely. Unfortunately, the richer he became, the more insufferable."

"So you divorced him," Clint said. "Where does that leave you now?"

"Here. I have a nice settlement. I'm comfortable."

"But not content."

"No," she said, placing her hand on his forearm. "I feel suffocated. He's insanely jealous of other men and continues to believe he owns me. I kept praying that someone would come along and beat him. And when you arrived, I thought my prayers had been answered."

"What do you think now?"

Her hand slid from his forearm to his thigh. "I haven't changed my mind."

Clint swallowed noisily. "So what are we going to do about it?"

Her eyelashes fluttered. "Pay Old Sid five dollars to walk around the block a time or two," she breathed.

Clint glanced over at the ancient hotel clerk. "He'll do that?"

"For five dollars . . . he'd do almost anything."

Clint nodded and walked over to the desk. The old fellow's head was nodding and it was clear he was struggling hard to keep his eyes open. "Take a walk on me," Clint said, laying a five-dollar bill on the counter. "Take a *long* walk."

Old Sid came awake fast. His skinny, liver-blotched hand darted out like the head of a snapping turtle and the money vanished into his pocket. "Thankee, thankee!" he chirped, dashing for the front door. "A long walk it will be! Thankee, thankee!"

Clint watched the door close and then he turned to see Vicki pulling off her gown right in the lobby. "Here?"

She nodded. "I can't wait. Can you?"

Clint hurried over to her side. She was already half undressed and when she slipped out of her chemise and stood before him wearing nothing but a pair of high heels, he damn near burst the buttons of his Levi's. She was gorgeous! Better even than he'd expected. Her breasts were the size and shape of golden cantaloupes, and when he bent forward and took one of her hard nipples in his mouth, they were every bit as sweet.

Vicki moaned. Fumbled for the buttons of his shirt. Outside, two men tromped by on the boardwalk only a few feet away, but they didn't look through the window, thank heavens.

"I can't believe we're going to do this right out here in the lobby for anyone to see who comes in or out or even looks through the window."

"I can," she panted. "I've always wanted it like this. I think. . . . ohh, don't, please hurry!"

Clint had pulled back and now he was tearing off his shirt and kicking off his boots. There was a big Persian rug on the floor that looked soft but Vicki shook her head and whispered, "The couch. Hurry!"

Clint hurried. He was long and hard and when he eased the passionate woman down, she draped one leg over the back of the couch and left the other on the floor. He reached down and stroked the wetness between her legs and she rotated her hips.

"How long will Old Sid be gone?" he gasped.

"Not long enough." She grabbed his rod and pulled him as if he were on a stout leash. "Come on!"

Clint gave himself up to the fact that there was to be no preliminaries. No foreplay. What Vicki Flowers wanted was the Gunsmith inside her and he was fully prepared to satisfy. When he slammed his throbbing member into her, she cried out with pleasure, and her head began to roll back and forth on the couch. "Oh, yes!" she wailed. "Yes. Yes!"

Clint's hard body rocked in and out. He was rather off-balance, with one foot on the floor and the other knee resting on the back of the sofa. It would have been better on the Persian rug but he was determined to make the best of the situation and Vicki seemed plenty happy.

Her hips were moving faster and faster and Clint felt as if he was being milked. As their bodies pistoned in and out of each other, Vickie's heel made tap music on the floor but neither of them noticed. She was a fabulous lover and every time Clint thought he was going to explode, she somehow stopped him until the sweet pain in his testicles was unbearable.

"Now!" she cried. "Do it now!"

Clint was more than ready. He felt Vicki's soft little body start to buck up and down and he heard the cry of ecstasy building up in her throat. Letting loose, he drove himself into her so frantically that the couch spilled over backward and they toppled onto the floor and thrashed until they were spent and gasping for air.

Old Sid began to giggle from behind the counter.

Clint pulled himself out of the nearly unconscious woman. "Damn you!" he growled. "You were supposed to take a *long* walk!"

"For me, it was long," the old fool cackled as he looked down at them. "Boy, I sure hope you two didn't break that couch up. Boss'll kill me if you did."

"And I'll shoot your eyes out if you don't drop back down behind that counter and pretend you can't hear or see anything!"

Old Sid disappeared. And under Clint, Vicki Flowers, stroked Clint's manhood and sighed with vast contentment.

FOUR

Clint and Vicki finished making love on a bed of grass a mile north of Cheyenne just in time to watch the sunrise pour like liquid gold across the Wyoming plains.

"I don't often see the sunrise," Vicki confessed. "In fact, this is the first time since I can remember. I like them even better than sunsets. I like *beginnings*, Clint."

He knew there was some personal meaning to her emphasis on the word "beginnings." He supposed she meant that she hoped that *they* were a new beginning. Clint frowned. "Vicki, everything in my life happens sudden, or so it seems. I guess what happened last night in the lobby was as sudden as anything I did in a long time."

"What about just now?"

"That wasn't sudden at all," he admitted, the smell of their lovemaking still fresh in his nostrils. "It was wonderful."

She squeezed his hand. "Clint, there was something I did want to discuss with you last night."

He was afraid she was going to suggest that they get married or some such thing but Vicki surprised him.

"I wanted to tell you that Max won't let you leave Cheyenne without a chance at getting even. He swears he would have beat you if you hadn't pulled him off Iron

Soldier. He's sending telegrams to all the newspapers publically challenging you to a thousand-mile race. Winner take all."

Clint damned near laughed outright. "A what?"

"A thousand-mile race," she repeated, quite seriously. "He means it, Clint! He's got it fixed in his mind that he can dethrone a legend by publicly humiliating you and Duke. He's got a flair for the dramatic and he knows that this will definitely catch the public's fancy. He means to push at this thing until you *have* to race him."

"I don't have to do anything I don't want! I'll just ignore the man and his newspaper stories and take the next train to Reno like I've been planning all along."

"You mean . . . you mean you'd leave me here so soon?"

The hurt in her voice filled the Gunsmith with guilt. "Listen," he said. "If you'd like to come along, I have some money and you have that big divorce settlement. We could go on over to San Francisco or even up to Tahoe. We could swim, make love on the warm sand, and watch the fish swim in the clear waters. You'd love it, Vicki."

"I'm sure I would," she told him. "But we'd have no peace. You just don't understand Max Holloway. He won't quit badgering you until you agree to race from here to Carson City."

Clint snorted with derision. "So that's the race, huh? Across a thousand miles of hard country. Deserts. Indians. No water, too much water. This time of year will be hotter than hell."

"He knows that. He rode for the Pony Express and he's never forgotten it. It was the highlight of his life and mostly what he talks about. I swear, if it wasn't for telegraphs and railroads, he'd *still* be a Pony Express rider."

"He's crazy!"

"Clint, won't you do it?"

"Are you crazy, too?"

She shrank back from him. "You can't mean that."

"No," he said, a tone of conciliation creeping into his voice. "I didn't. It's just that this whole subject is nonsense."

"But you were going to Reno anyway. You said so. Carson City is just a few miles south."

"Yeah, but I was going to put Duke in a boxcar and myself in a coach and ride the train to the Sierras. Not enter some insane thousand-mile race."

Vicki stood up and climbed into her underclothes and her gown, which she buttoned all the way up to her chin. "I think that kind of horse race would be history in the making," she said in almost a pout. "I'd be so proud of you if you won."

"Well, I'm damned sorry. But if I have to kill Duke or get killed to make you proud, then never mind. The whole idea is nuts. I won't change my mind."

Vicki pulled on her high-heeled shoes and whirled away from him to start walking back to Cheyenne. "I thought you were a man who liked excitement," she called back to him. "I know your horse can beat Iron Soldier, so that isn't the reason. What's wrong with you? Lost your famous nerve?"

The accusation did not deserve a response, so Clint pulled on his clothes, then laid back down on the grass and felt the rising sun warm his skin. The Union Pacific was due in to Cheyenne tomorrow afternoon and he'd be on it when it left a few hours later. He was sorry that Vicki had been so upset by his refusal to take part in Holloway's ridiculous race and sure that the man simply sought publicity for Iron Soldier and fame for himself, which he would capitalize on to make more money. Well, let him think of some other hare-brained scheme.

• • •

"Say, Mr. Adams!" a man yelled as Clint trudged into Cheyenne, his hair mussed and his eyes bloodshot from lack of sleep. "When will the race begin and what kind of odds do you give yourself against a man with enough money to buy whatever edge he needs?"

Clint rubbed his whiskery face. "Who are you?"

"I'm a reporter from the *Cheyenne Daily*. I got Mr. Holloway's story all about how you cheated on that race yesterday. But he sure is looking forward to the big one."

"There won't be any 'big' one! I'm not going to race."

The man frowned. "He's telling everyone you'd say that at first, but later you'd change your mind when you learned that he was offering five-to-one odds against all takers that he'd cross the finish line at least ten miles ahead of you."

"Max Holloway said that?"

The reporter nodded. Flipped open a little notebook and thumbed through it rapidly until he found the exact quote he wanted. "That's right. Said it right here. Also said that your horse is fast, but he hasn't the heart for a big race. He said Duke would quit after a couple of hundred miles."

Clint snorted in anger. "That fool sure does seem to know a lot about my horse. But then, I guess he ought to, he's saw enough of its ass end when we raced the last time."

The reporter barked a humorless laugh and scribbled down the quote. "Very funny, Mr. Adams. But the truth of the matter is, Mr. Holloway is dead serious. And I'm just afraid that, when the train comes rolling in from the East, there will be a bunch of newspaper reporters asking you all the same questions. So I implore you, give me a scoop. An exclusive interview on just how you plan to win that race."

Clint was starting to get very annoyed. "I just got through telling you that I won't do it! Now write that down in your little notebook and go away. I need some food and some sleep."

The reporter looked past him and clucked his tongue. "What would you say if I printed the fact that I saw Miss Flowers come walking into Cheyenne a few minutes ago? Grass in her hair, probably grass stains on her shapely butt. She looked almost as tired as you do. You must have had—"

Clint's fist smashed into the man's teeth. The reporter's notebook flew out of his hands and the man went down hard. Clint stood over him and said, "Print anything about me and Miss Flowers and you're hospital bound. Understand me?"

The man had both hands over his mouth and blood seeped between his fingers. He nodded his head but there was hatred in his eyes. Clint walked on. He was thinking that the best thing he could do would be to pack his gear and ride west to Laramie after taking a good long nap. He could catch the train there and avoid all this insanity.

Yes, he decided, that's exactly what I will do.

When he got to his hotel room, Clint kicked off his boots and eased down on his bed. He was angry and frustrated. He'd gotten enough of Miss Flowers to know he wanted some more despite the fact she'd wounded his pride when she'd angrily accused him of losing his nerve. Of course, that was nonsense. Clint had proved his courage time and time again. But still, the words hurt.

Max Holloway was another annoyance. The man seemed intent on tearing down the Gunsmith to build himself and Iron Soldier up bigger than they deserved. If Clint rode on to Laramie, a lot of people just might believe he'd been afraid he'd lose that crazy thousand-mile horse race. To hell with them! The whole idea was the product of a warped mind.

Clint closed his eyes. He saw the vision of Vicki Flowers and a smile creased his lips. What a woman! What a—

"Open up!" a voice shouted. "Mr. Adams, are you in there?"

Clint pulled his gun and reluctantly eased his feet off the bed. "Who is it?"

"Sheriff Paine. Shorty Evans has been beaten and robbed. He's in bad shape and calling your name."

"Damn!" Clint swore as he charged the door and opened it with his gun still in his fist. Seeing that it really was the sheriff, Clint holstered his gun and grabbed his boots. "Is he going to live?"

"The doctor isn't sure. It's touch and go. I guess old Shorty must think an awful damn lot of you Gunsmith. After whiskey, you're the only thing he asked for."

A wry grin touched the corners of Clint's mouth. "Then I'm flattered," he said, pulling on his boots and grabbing his black Stetson. "Any idea of who did this?"

"Not a clue. Happened sometime early this morning. They found Shorty about eight o'clock back in the alley. Somebody damn near caved his skull in. If he hadn't been wearing that old floppy campaign hat he likes, his brains would already be scrambled."

Clint said nothing more until they reached the doctor's office. He pushed into the room where Shorty was laid out with a massive bandage wrapped around and around his skull. Shorty's face was also battered blue. "Some sonofabitch really worked him over, didn't they?" Clint said between gritted teeth.

The doctor nodded. He was a tall, spare man with a silver goatee and watery eyes behind a pair of bifocals. He looked owlish and competent. "They sure did. He's got a bad concussion. Maybe some real brain damage, though I think he was already brain-damaged from spilling off so many

WINNER TAKE ALL

broncs for all those years. He's going to need some very close watching over, Mr. Adams."

"The hell with that noise," Shorty growled, his eyes trying to peek out from under the huge swelling of his eyelids. "I can take care of myself."

"How?" the doctor asked.

Shorty's eyes filled with tears he could not hide. "I'll make do," he spat. "It ain't nobody's problem but my own."

Clint heaved a long sigh. "You saved my life once. I'm not about to leave you down and out like this."

Shorty tried to shake his head in protest but the effort brought such pain he screwed his face up and groaned.

"What shall I do with him?" the doctor asked.

"We'll take him over to my hotel and I'll put him in my room until he gets better."

"Might be a couple of weeks."

"I'll stay as long as it takes."

The doctor managed a tired smile. "You're known to be mighty good with a gun, but I never heard you was also a hell of a friend."

"So was Shorty in his good days," Clint said. "Anything more you can do with him here?"

"Nope. I'll stop by to visit him twice a day until I'm sure he's on the road to recovery."

Clint bent down and picked the old broncobuster up and carried him out the door. So much for his plan to escape to Laramie tonight. He guessed this meant he was just going to have to remain in Cheyenne and face Holloway's challenge and all the nosy reporters that were supposed to show up on the train.

Sometimes, nothing went as it was supposed to.

FIVE

Clint heard the westbound Union Pacific roll into Cheyenne, and he said a little prayer that Vicki had been wrong when she said that there would be a horde of eastern newspaper reporters descending upon him.

"You might as well give in and do 'er," Shorty groaned from the bed. "You got no choice now. Holloway will hound you until you cave in."

"That's what everyone keeps saying," Clint replied. "But I can be pretty stubborn once my mind is made up. And in this case, it's made up."

Shorty frowned and winced because he kept forgetting that frowning caused him pain. "I don't understand your reasoning. You stand to make a fortune by accepting the challenge. And even if you lose, you could make it up at some other horse race. Why, you might even make more money in the long run if you lost. That way, people wouldn't be so afraid of racing you."

"I'm just not interested in being a racing promoter," Clint said. "My trade is gunsmithing and I like to make a little money at faro and poker. I'm not driven to get rich. I enjoy having fun too much."

"Well," Shorty said with a sad shake of his head. "I

guess when you get to be my age, all the fun is squeezed out of you and what you want is enough money to ease your bones down in a soft chair and rock the last days of your life away. I like a nice cat in my lap and a warm fire to gaze into on cold days."

Clint didn't say anything. He wasn't particularly fond of cats, though he'd seen a few he thought deserved to live. Mostly, he liked women, guns, cards, and horses. The things almost every man liked.

Clint pulled the drapes aside and gazed down at the street. After a few minutes, he watched the train pull into the station. Almost at once, passengers began to unload. A lot of passengers. Clint saw a bunch of young men come bustling off the station platform. They got directions from the conductor and headed for town. "Here they come," he said bitterly. "I can tell a newspaper reporter as quick as I can a gambler or a thief. I'm in trouble."

Even as Clint watched, Max Holloway came riding up on Iron Soldier, as big and as shiny as the summer sun. He was dressed in white right down to his boots and his gray horse wore a silver breastcollar. Clint had to admit that they made a fine sight, as fine as the Mexican vaqueros and their spirited horses at a fiesta.

"I can just imagine what he's telling them," Clint muttered to himself as the reporters crowded around Max Holloway, dropped their bags in the dirt of the street, and reached for the notepads as if they were going for their guns.

"He's telling them that you cheated him and that the two fastest horses in the West ought to have a go at each other," Shorty said. "He's tellin' 'em of the challenge he made and how you never backed away from a gunbattle in your life, but now you're backing down from him."

"How do you know what he's saying?"

" 'Cause he told me," Shorty replied. "We had a drink last night. A couple of drinks. I tried to buy, but he wouldn't hear of it."

"But the man fired you!"

"I know. But I've learned not to burn any bridges. I figured maybe he wanted to hire me back."

"You've lost your senses. I gave you enough money to last a long time."

"I need to be doing something with horses. Besides Iron Soldier, Holloway has some of the finest horses in the country. Horses bred to run and to work cattle. I had a part in setting up his breeding program. To me, those horses are even more important than my own life. They *are* my life."

Clint could understand that. But it still didn't excuse the fact that Shorty should have used a whole lot more sense than to let a man like Max Holloway know that he had money. To do such a thing was to invite disaster. "I don't suppose he happened to notice you were buying drinks like you had plenty of money."

"He mighta."

"Why, sure he did!" Clint swung away from the window. "I'll bet you most anything that he's the one that arranged for you to be beaten and robbed."

"But he don't need my money!"

"No, but he must have reasoned I'd stick around if you were hurt. The money was just sugar-coating. He wanted me to stay in Cheyenne. And it worked."

Shorty lapsed into a brooding silence.

"Aw, hell," Clint sighed. "It wasn't your fault. It was mine. I should have gone and put a stop to this nonsense the moment it started. So I guess that's what I'll do right now."

Shorty tried to sit up. "Don't you lose your temper and gun him down, Clint! With all those reporters standing around the man, you'll be sure to hang."

Clint strapped on his six-gun. He peered out the window just before he grabbed his hat off the bedpost and saw Holloway pointing up toward his hotel window. There must have been thirty or forty reporters down there and they were all staring up at Clint. When they saw him looking down at them, they rushed toward the hotel. Clint swung around and went out to head them off. He meant to end this business once and for all.

He met the pack of reporters on the stairway leading up to his second-floor room. "That's far enough," he shouted, drawing his gun and firing a shot directly over their heads and into the ceiling.

The reporters whirled and stampeded back down, some of them practically crawling over the slower ones down below. They hit the base of the stairs in a pile, and Clint followed them down.

Holstering his gun, he said, "I know why your newspapers sent you to Cheyenne, but I'm here to say that you've been tricked into a wasted trip. I'm not racing a thousand miles across the plains and the deserts. Any sane man would refuse such a ridiculous challenge."

"But, sir!" a man yelled, "I'm from the *Omaha Star* and this could be the greatest story of the decade! Why, our editors are all waiting breathlessly beside the telegraph to file this one."

"They can wait all they want," Clint said. "The fact of the matter is, I already raced my horse against Iron Soldier and won."

"You cheated!" Max Holloway yelled, as he stormed through the crowd of reporters with two of his gunmen on either side of him. "You knocked me from my horse and prevented me from winning."

Clint's voice hardened. "I was passing you when you quirted my black's nose. The next time you slashed him across the eyes, so I grabbed your own quirt and used it to haul you out of the saddle."

"That's not true!"

Clint had to grip the banister to keep from jumping forward and grabbing Holloway by the throat. "You had every advantage, including a horse trained to make a hairpin turn around a tree. I still won."

"Iron Soldier could whip your horse in a long race," Holloway said. "And I'm a better horseman than you ever thought of being."

Clint wasn't in the mood to argue. "You can say or think that, it doesn't matter to me. What I want is to prove you almost had Shorty Evans killed so I'd stick around Cheyenne."

"I don't know what you're talking about."

"Somehow, Max, I had a feeling you'd say that. And I guess that I have no proof or chance of getting any proof, so—"

"I challenge you to a horse race!" Max yelled, interrupting Clint. "I challenge you to the greatest horse race of all time. A thousand miles, winner take all, no holds barred. Why won't you accept?"

"Because I'm not willing to risk the health of my horse for money. You shouldn't be, either."

Max Holloway wagged his head back and forth. "No, that's not the *real* reason you won't race. The real reason is that you and that horse of yours are both too soft and spineless to withstand the rigors and adversities we'd face."

Clint's knuckles whitened on the banister. "If I raced you, it would be against all your advantages of money and men."

"That's not true. It would be man against man. Horse

against horse in the ultimate test. We'll race along the tracks," he said. "I believe these gentlemen and their employers would petition the railroad to provide a special train to accompany us. The train would also ensure we had good food, a bed to rest in, and protection from the Indians. The train would insure that it was a fair race."

The newspaper reporters began to babble with excitement. One of them said, "Yeah, I'm sure we could pool our expense money and do that. The eyes of America would be on us. We could all file our stories at the telegraph offices along the transcontinental route. It would be fine."

"How about it, Mr. Adams?"

"What are the odds?"

"Five-to-one."

"Make them ten-to-one and we have a horse race," Clint said, hating himself for changing his mind but unable to allow Max Holloway a shred of glory to be made of this challenge.

"Those are unconscionable odds! Why, I wouldn't give them to a man if he were riding a milk cow!"

The reporters broke into nervous laughter but Clint was not amused. "Then to hell with it," he said, as he started to turn away and head up the stairs to his room.

"Wait!" Holloway yelled. "Seven-to-one and to the victor goes all the spoils of a sweet victory."

Clint turned and was about to ask what the "spoils" were when he saw Vicki being shoved forward. She turned her face up to him and smiled. Their eyes met and Clint swallowed with desire. He thought about how nice it would be to take Vicki to Tahoe and then the Barbary Coast with about seven thousand dollars of Max Holloway's money in his pockets.

"You got a deal," he said. "As soon as Shorty is ready, I'm ready, too."

Max Holloway clapped his hands together and grinned. "Excellent!" he cried. "We'll make history and give this country a show like it's never seen or will see again!"

Clint nodded. Vicki winked. The reporters cheered and raced off to the telegraph office to file the first of their exciting great horse race stories.

SIX

The telegraph lines hummed until dawn that night as the reporters filed their stories across the nation. The following day, people from New York to Savannah, Georgia, were talking about the race and the news story was splashed across all the West Coast papers as well. The idea of a race pitting two famed horses and a legendary ex-lawman thrown in to spice things up, was just too exciting to be ignored.

Max Holloway wanted to delay the race for a few weeks in order to build up anticipation to a fever pitch, but Clint was adamant in his insistence that the race would begin as soon as possible, possible meaning as soon as he was sure he could leave Shorty Evans.

"The hell with that noise!" Shorty cried, tearing the bandages off his head and standing up. "I'm taking the train west and I'll be your manager. I'll see that Duke has fresh feed and water and that he's curried and taken care of."

Clint studied the old broncbuster. "Are you sure you're up to the task? Even before you were beat up and robbed, you were in pretty bad shape."

"If you're asking me if I'll stay sober and take care of business, the answer is, yes!"

"All right," Clint said. "That's good enough for me. I got to have someone on board that train that I can trust and you're it. I guess the way it's to work is that the train stays with the leader."

"What about the woman? You ain't going to trust her, are you?"

"You mean Miss Flowers?"

"I mean Mrs. Victoria Holloway!" Shorty groused.

"She's divorced."

"Are you sure about that?"

"I know she lives alone at the Transcontinental Hotel. Why should she lie?"

"Makes you wonder, doesn't it?" Shorty asked. "I don't know if she's lying. All I got to say is that you've been sort of mooning around here and it's plain to see that little witch has got a spell cast over you. It'd take a saint to ignore her, but I wouldn't trust a woman who'd been married to the man who was trying to beat me and my horse into the ground."

"I haven't seen her alone since the first night we met."

"She'll be around," Shorty predicted. "The word is out that she almost shot Max Holloway a couple evenings ago at the fancy restaurant you like. They got into a real fight, and he belted her in the eye. She pulled a derringer and people dove under their tables. A shot was fired, but she missed."

Clint laughed outright. "She did that to him?"

"That's what I heard. While you were out exercising Duke yesterday, a couple of my old friends came up to visit. They say that there will be even more reporters arriving on the next train west."

"There's too many already," Clint said. "The best thing we can do is to get this race started and finished."

Shorty nodded carefully. "I'll drink to that."

"No, you won't," Clint said. "If I win, I'll buy you the finest whiskey money can buy. We'll celebrate in Virginia City and Lake Tahoe both."

WINNER TAKE ALL 43

"But I got to stop drinking until then?"

"That's the deal, old-timer."

Shorty nodded. His hand trembled a little as he stuck it out and they shook on the agreement. Shorty said, "I wouldn't do this for another livin' soul. Besides, to see those two horses run day after day, why, I'll roll naked in cactus for a week if that's what was asked."

Clint patted the old man's shoulder. "You just take care of Duke when he needs it. I'll take care of myself."

"You'd better watch your back," Shorty said. "If you start pulling away from Holloway, he'll find a way to cut you down."

Clint agreed. Even strangers who liked the idea of his being such an underdog were starting to warn him that Max Holloway was diabolical enough to come up with every trick imaginable.

Clint went downstairs where there were always at least a half-dozen reporters lounging around in the lobby. "That special U.P. your newspapers ordered to follow the race comes through tomorrow," he told them all. "There will be more of you fellas on board and it's going to get mighty crowded around here if we don't get this race started. That's why I'm starting as soon as the train arrives."

The newspaper reporters were on their feet all at once. "But Mr. Holloway had ordered a special new saddle, and a veterinarian from Kentucky is on his way to tend to Iron Soldier. What about—"

Clint cut the arguments short. "I'm riding out tomorrow with or without Holloway and Iron Soldier. I'm not waiting another day in Cheyenne. I figure Max Holloway will decide that he has no choice but to start, too. End of discussion."

"Hey!" Holloway shouted, as he hurried across the street to catch the Gunsmith emerging from the livery stable where he had just spent some time graining and overseeing a blacksmith put new shoes on Duke. "Wait just a damned minute!"

Clint stopped and watched as Holloway and a pack of newspaper reporters stormed across the street. The Gunsmith knew that there was going to be an argument.

Holloway stopped right in Clint's face. He was a few inches taller than the Gunsmith and ruggedly handsome in a wolfish sort of way. "What's this about the race starting tomorrow?" he demanded. "We've got more reporters coming next week and my special veterinarian and—"

"We've waited to get this thing going too long already," Clint said. "Tomorrow's train arrives at two o'clock in the afternoon and that's when the race starts."

"No!" Holloway shouted. "We leave when I say we leave and not before. I've put too much effort into this for you to jump the gun and ruin the second greatest event ever staged across a thousand miles of the rugged frontier."

"The first being the Pony Express?"

"That's right," Holloway said gravely. "There will never be anything like it."

He turned to the reporters who hovered around them and launched into one of his oft-repeated stories. "There was a time, during what is now known as the Paiute Indian War, when I was forced to ride three hundred miles across hostile Indian lands for five straight days in the saddle without . . ."

As the pencils began to scratch furiously, Clint turned and walked away. He was leaving tomorrow and Holloway and the Iron Soldier could go or stay, it no longer mattered to him.

"Clint?"

He turned at the sound of a sweet, familiar voice. "Hello, Miss Flowers," he said. "How have you been?"

"Fine."

Facial makeup and a heavy layer of powder could not hide the dark smudge encircling her right eye where Max

Holloway's fist had landed. Anger, hot and quick flickered in Clint, but he let it pass and chose not to make an issue of it.

"Clint, I went up to your room to talk privately with you, but Shorty was there and he doesn't seem too fond of me."

"Oh," Clint said, taking the young woman's arm and walking along, "it's not a matter of being fond of you or not, it's just that he questions your loyalties. He's not sure who you are for and who you are against."

"Why, I'm for you!" She stamped her foot down on the boardwalk. "How could you question that after . . . well, after what we've already meant to each other."

"I don't know," he said. "Are you coming along to help me or Max?"

"You, of course! Clint, don't be mean with me! I do want to help you all that I can. In fact, I've decided to leave Cheyenne forever and go with you to that Lake . . . what did you call it?"

"Tahoe."

"Yes, well, it sounds cool and lovely and there is no one that I'd rather see it with for the first time than you."

"Is that a fact?" He was pleased. "Maybe you'd like to also have dinner with me and take another midnight walk out on the prairie."

"I have a better idea," she said. "I know a wonderful little room where we can be all to ourselves tonight without worrying about reporters or loose gossipers. It will be the last night we can spend together until we finish the race."

"I was planning to spend the night in the stall next to Duke."

"You'll spend plenty of nights with that horse. Tonight *will* be special."

Clint looked down into her lovely, upturned face. He was aware that they were being watched by reporters and everyone else out on the street so he did not take her into his arms, but it was an effort.

Yet, later that night as they stood alone in a small room and undressed each other, breathless with anticipation, Clint knew that she was worth the wait. In the flickering kerosene lamplight, he held her close and stroked her buttocks and thighs, kissed her hard nipples, and listened to her moan with pleasure.

"You're going to beat Max," she sighed as he picked her up and carried her to the bed. "You're going to win!"

Clint did not want to talk about the race. All he wanted was to lose himself in her body and so he spread her legs apart and buried his rigid penis in her.

Vicki wrapped her legs around his waist and her little bottom began to pump energetically as she whispered, "This beats the horsehair couch all to hell, doesn't it, Clint."

"It sure does!" he grunted, moving powerfully in and out of her, building them both to a climax.

When he came, she cried out with pleasure and seconds later, her own body began to jerk and buck. She clawed at his back and her tongue filled his mouth and her sleek thighs gripped him like a vise until she relaxed and lay spent and satisfied.

"Have we got a night ahead of us," she panted, looking up at him with her large, feline eyes.

Clint agreed. He had no idea of how long it would take to reach Carson City, but this night was sure going to give him an incentive to make the race as brief as possible.

SEVEN

Clint, Shorty, and Vicki Flowers stood together inside the livery stable, and they could hear the Union Pacific train's whistle blasts. There was a big crowd outside and somewhere out there, Max Holloway and his small army of race support people were preparing Iron Soldier for the run of his life.

The Gunsmith was grim-faced and all business. He was having regrets about getting into this match in the first place, and he wished he had gone to Laramie as he'd originally planned. But then, there had been Shorty's concussion and last night with Vicki. But even that had come with a price. Max Holloway had probably gone to bed early and gotten a full night's sleep, while Clint. . . . Well, he was still young and randy enough that he did not always bend to good sense when it came to beautiful women.

Shorty was very serious, too. "The thing is," he said. "You got to pace yourself all the way. My advice is not to worry about getting out in front of Holloway, but just keeping him in sight. Duke is the better horse, and if you're close at the finish, you'll win."

"I won't risk his health," Clint vowed. "If this horse starts to show signs of having difficulty, I'll just quit the race and forfeit the thousand dollars. I'd rather have Duke sound than all the money in Cheyenne."

Vicki stroked Duke's nose. "He's such a beautiful animal. I'm sure that he can win without hurting himself."

Clint heard the crowd starting to call his name. He'd vowed to leave when the train arrived and it was time to go. He tightened his cinch, made a final check of the lightweight saddlebags he'd bought, which were crammed with a blanket, jerked beef, extra ammunition, and a pair of army binoculars. He also had a few horseshoe nails, a canteen, and a map of Nevada. If he fell behind, he planned to cut southwest across the state. By ducking south of Reno and taking a more direct line, he guessed he could chop off about a hundred miles. Trouble was, if he did that, he'd be leaving the protection of the train and striking across the heart of the Paiute country. It was risky, but he'd do it if necessary.

"Let's get this thing started," he said.

Vicki hugged his neck and kissed him passionately.

"Dammit!" Shorty swore. "Shall I take the horse outside so you two can fall down in the straw and use the last of your strength? We're running a race and you both look tired as hell before we're even started!"

Clint pulled away from Vicki. "Sorry," he said to her, "but Shorty's right. It's a good thing I can sleep in the saddle at night. And I'll do that."

"Max can, too," she said.

"He told you that?"

She nodded. "Lots of times. In fact, he had custom-made straps that will hold him upright while he rides. Made them special for this race."

Shorty groused. "Hell, I wouldn't be surprised if he hires a couple of men to ride along on each side of him to hold him up while he sleeps, feed him while he's hungry, wipe his—"

"That's enough," Clint said. "Let's get this thing started. I didn't agree to this race with the thought of losing. Holloway can get all the help he wants, but it still comes down to one horse and one man that has to cover every mile."

Clint tightened the cinch and mounted Duke. As if the gelding understood that he was about to begin his greatest test, Duke shivered with expectancy while Shorty and Vicki opened the barn doors.

At the sight of the Gunsmith on his beautifully curried and tended horse, the crowd broke into applause. But it was a small crowd, no more than thirty, and Clint realized that all the others were waiting for the big race favorite, Iron Soldier.

"The odds on the street are seven-to-one against you!" a man called to the Gunsmith. "I took 'em and so did the rest of us. Don't let us down."

Clint studied the expectant faces and felt a need to explain his own reservations. "If this horse goes lame or tires badly, I'll drop out of the race. I won't cripple him, so you better understand that. I got a feeling that Holloway will run Iron Soldier to death, if that's what it takes. Maybe that gives him an even bigger advantage than the odds. I don't know. But I just figured you folks ought to understand how I feel right now, so that no one can accuse me of throwing the race."

"Now just wait a damn minute!" a freighter called. "All of us put down hard money on you and that horse. You *better* finish and win."

"Mister, if you want your money on a man that will kill his horse to win, then bet on Holloway."

The freighter flushed with anger. "Goddammit, then I will."

He stomped away to change his bet around and took about half the little throng of supporters with him. A hard-used sodbuster in frayed overalls and worn-out boots eased up to Duke and gave the horse a couple of cubes of sugar. "Mister Adams, I saw you race this horse in Denver four years ago and I also saw you face three men in a gunfight down in Del Rio, Texas. You can say what you want, but I know that you're no quitter. Holloway will have to kill you and this animal if he expects to get to Carson City first. I'm betting three hundred dollars—every last cent of my wheat seed money—on you to win. So are a couple of my friends and their families."

"I wish you hadn't done that," Clint said quitely. He realized full well that the man was saying he would be financially ruined if Duke lost.

"You'll win," the man's wife said, stepping forward with a little boy in tow. "Around these parts, Mr. Holloway fancies himself the next thing to God. He's run horses and cattle over our crops and threatened anyone who rubs him the wrong way. He rides that horse across our fields and looks down at us like we was dirt."

The woman's voice shook. "You beat him, Mr. Adams! You make him eat crow and cost him that prideful way he has toward everybody who has less'n he does! Take him down a peg."

Clint nodded. "What's your son's name?"

"Peter."

Clint bent down from his saddle and stretched out his hand. "How old are you, Pete?"

"Seven," came the whispered reply as the boy shyly touched the Gunsmith's hand.

"Did you bet anything on me?"

"Ain't got no money," he said, trying hard to meet Clint's eye. "But if I had some, I'd bet it on you!"

Clint dug a silver-dollar out of his pants pocket and handed it to the boy. "You bet this and I promise that you'll get seven more just like it back in a week."

The boy stared in round-eyed wonder at the silver dollar. Obviously, he'd never had such a prize. "It's mine?"

"It's yours. You can buy candy, a pocket knife, or whatever you want."

"He's bettin' it on you, Mr. Adams," the woman said with her chin held high. "Jest like me and my husband are betting our seed money and farm on you."

Clint straightened in the saddle and rode away with the boy's face etched in his mind. The sodbuster had been right—he was going to win and he'd do everything short of hurting Duke to do it.

They met beside the train's hissing locomotive. Max Holloway shouted something, but Clint couldn't hear the man over the sound of the steam and the huge crowd. He spotted Shorty and Vicki in the crowd. They'd be taking this train along with all the newspaper reporters and a small army of helpers on Holloway's payroll. Clint was as concerned about Shorty and Vicki's safety as he was about Duke's. The odd pair were going to be crucial to his own victory. They'd have food and feed readied, help him in any way they could. If he started to win, Clint had little doubt that they'd become easy targets, and with him on Duke's back, he wouldn't be able to help them.

Max Holloway rode up on Iron Soldier, and he was a sight. He wore a real Pony Express saddle with its famed *mochila*, thought it was practically empty and obviously more for show than anything else. He carried no rifle, but only a pearl-handled revolver, and he was dressed in tailor-made buckskins that had never seen a campfire. He pulled off his Stetson and waved it to the crowd, and they cheered the man they'd betted on to win. Iron Soldier looked unbeatable. His coat was so shiny from brushing that he looked as if he were made of polished pewter. He pranced and threw his head to the crowd like a politician on campaign.

The crowd separated and a wide swath opened itself to lead straight west along the railroad tracks. Then two men unwound a red ribbon between them, and Clint and Max Holloway rode up side by side.

"You ever see anything the likes of this!" Holloway shouted. "Look at it! Reporters are here from all over the country. Would have been a hell of a lot more if we'd have waited another two weeks. We had telegrams saying that the French and the English wanted to come!"

"We've got enough," Clint growled, steadying Duke.

Suddenly, Holloway whirled Iron Soldier around as if to realign himself for the start and the horse took the opportunity to strike out with his back feet. Clint felt Duke take the blows on his shoulder.

"Damn you!" he shouted, jumping off the gelding to inspect the shoulder.

Shorty was right beside him, and they both groaned when they saw that Iron Soldier's hooves had torn flesh. Probably muscle, too.

"I'll get some liniment," Shorty said, rushing away.

Clint blotted the injury with a clean bandanna. He led Duke forward, and the animal showed that he was in pain by favoring the shoulder.

Max yelled, "Sorry about that! Maybe we should wait after all."

Clint said nothing because he didn't trust himself to speak. He knew enough about horses to keep Duke moving so that the shoulder did not stiffen up and lame the horse. Shorty rushed back with liniment and rubbed a generous amount of it into Duke's injured shoulder. "I think he's going to be better off if you keep him moving. Movement is the only thing that will keep the swelling down."

"I heartily disagree!" a man said, pushing his way in to touch the shoulder. "This is a bad contusion. The horse needs at least a week to rest and—"

"Who the hell are you?" Clint demanded.

"He's Holloway's own veterinarian," Shorty spat.

Clint grabbed the man by the shirt and hurled him into the crowd. He bent back to Shorty. "What do *you* say?"

"Get on him and ride him around a minute or two. If he don't limp, then race. But start real slow and easy. No more than a trot."

"A trot?"

"That's right. It's the best gait anyway over a long distance. Never mind what the crowd will do. Just trot nice and easy until you're sure that Duke will be fine."

"I'll do that," Clint said, swinging into the saddle and reining Duke into a wide circle while the crowd clamored for him to take him to the starting line.

Shorty was bent over, hands on his knees, intently studying every motion of Duke's front end. When he was satisfied, he nodded his head and waved his hand in a circle that ended pointing west.

Clint heaved a sigh of relief. He trusted Shorty's knowledge of horses better than any veterinarian's. Clint rode back to the starting line.

"You're a fool to start now," Holloway growled.

Clint rode in close. Iron Soldier squealed and his teeth flashed at Duke's neck, but this time, the gelding was ready and bit into horseflesh first even as the back of Clint's hand struck Holloway across the mouth and bloodied his lips.

Holloway's men pushed forward but the starter wisely raised his weapon and everyone froze with anticipation. Even the huge locomotive seemed to hush its rhythmic panting.

Clint blocked everything out of his mind except the race

and the line of glistening steel rails that stretched out ahead of him. They ran together far, far on the western horizon. The starter raised his gun and the shot sent Iron Soldier leaping forward. The big stallion was racing as if it were only going one mile.

Clint had to fight to hold Duke in and make him trot off in an easy way that made the crowd hoot with derision. But the hoots soon faded and even the train's shrill whistle grew faint in the Gunsmith's ear as he trotted along after the gray stallion which was widening its lead with every stride.

Clint knew he looked like a Sunday rider on a rented nag as he moved west. He would be the first to concede it was a damn poor beginning, but then, in a horse race, it was only the ending that counted.

EIGHT

Clint lost sight of Holloway and Iron Soldier. He could see the Laramie Mountains up ahead and he knew that Holloway would already have reached them and would be making the climb. That was all right with him, because the most important thing was that Duke was sound and that Iron Soldier's shod hooves had not caused a serious injury to the gelding. It was Clint's intention to go slow this day and then, tomorrow, test the gelding's shoulder with an easy gallop.

At dusk, the Union Pacific train overtook him and it slowed as the Gunsmith trotted steadily along the tracks. There were reporters hanging out of every car window, all on Clint's side. As the train came abreast of him, they were all asking the same question. Why didn't Clint pick up his speed? What kind of a horse race could he possibly make of it if he didn't put the spurs to that black gelding?

Clint ignored the reporters, and it was only when the train began to edge slowly ahead that Shorty and Vicki were brought even with him.

"How's he feel?" Shorty yelled.

"Feels strong and right as ever," Clint shouted over the clattering of the track.

Shorty studied the horse with all his concentration. "Let

him gallop a little so I can watch."

Clint gave Duke some rein and the gelding surged ahead of Shorty and Vicki. Duke felt like a thousand pounds of muscle knotted up and ready to explode. Clint pulled the horse back in and Duke chomped impatiently at the bit. "He knows he's losing this horse race."

Shorty grinned. "He's striding as pretty as ever. Let him extend himself, Clint. You got to make up some ground or you'll fall so far behind you'll never see Iron Soldier's dust again."

That was what the Gunsmith had really wanted to hear. The idea of spending the night monotonously trotting along some lonesome railroad tracks had seemed mighty unappealing. Again, he gave Duke his head and the horse responded with a tremendous surge of power as he outran the train. Reporters who had, only moments before, been calling to him with disgust, now cheered.

Clint let the gelding run free for five miles, and then he settled him down into an easy gallop that would carry them right up to the Laramie Mountains. He knew that Duke would have to rest for a short spell and graze before climbing over the mountains and continuing on through the night but that was fine. Iron Soldier would have to do the same. Max Holloway might think he was reenacting the Pony Express, but there was one major difference he could not ignore without defeating himself, and that was that there were no relay stations with fresh horses every fifteen or twenty miles. Furthermore, Duke and Iron Soldier might be the finest horseflesh ever to run across the West, but they were only made out of flesh, blood, and bone. Flesh tore, blood spilled, and bones broke.

To Clint's way of thinking, this race was going to be tactical. The man who knew his horse and its limitations best, and the man who was lucky enough not to make too many mistakes, that was the man who was going to bring his horse across the finish line and win the bet.

Clint wondered if Holloway knew that as well.

Max Holloway could not help but look back over his shoulder even after it got dark. It was crazy, for he knew that he was miles ahead of the Gunsmith, maybe even as much as twenty miles. Three miles out of Cheyenne, he'd slowed Iron Soldier to a sensible gallop because the train was far behind and there was no need to put on a show.

That first night, he followed the tracks up and over the Laramies, and daybreak found him entering Laramie City with the Union Pacific train only a few miles behind. Max galloped right through the main street of town, but it was so early in the morning that the only people awake to see him were a few drunks and industrious storekeepers.

That was a real pity, Max thought, because the ones that did see him gallop past sure got an eyeful. He whipped off his white Stetson and let out a big hoo-ray at the startled citizens, and then he swept on through town wishing he'd have hit Laramie City about four hours later so that they could all have seen him in his new buckskin outfit—the kind he'd seen no less a man than Kit Carson himself wear while employed as a Pony Express rider. Oh, well, there were a whole lot of other rail towns that would get to see him race through, the next being Medicine Bow at the tail end of the Black Hills, and then Benton and Rawlins. Of course, none were as big as Cheyenne, but they'd do.

With the dawn creeping up behind him and making long shadows race Iron Soldier west, Max was reminded of a day years ago when he'd raced for his life from Indians on a Pony Express horse that had not been near Iron Soldier's equal. Of course, it had been fresher, but then, even tired, Iron Solider was far superior to almost any horse Max had ever ridden in those days. Back then, he'd been fifteen pounds lighter and in better shape. The Pony Express riders were mostly just kids, with Kit Carson and a few others being the exception. Kids as young as fifteen and whipcord thin and rawhide tough. God, it had been something! The greatest days of his life. But now, this was even better because he was the main attraction and of worldwide attention.

Max slowed Iron Soldier to a trot and turned in his saddle to see the train stop at Laramie City. He had memorized the distances between each rail town, and even between train stations, and also the arrival and departure times. At Laramie City, the Union Pacific would only take on fuel and water, change conductors and a few passengers before getting underway again. Max calculated that the train would overtake him before he reached Medicine Bow.

About two hours later when he came to a farmhouse, Max reined Iron Soldier to a standstill and dismounted. The stallion looked tired and his coat was matted with dried sweat and he seemed drawn up in the belly.

"I'm going to have to slow the pace down," he said to the horse as well as himself. "We can win this thing easy if you don't go lame. Hell, we can win it even if you *do* go lame! But don't tell anyone."

Max had taken the precaution of making sure that a dead-ringer for Iron Soldier was on the Union Pacific train hidden from view in a locked cattle car along with about thirty cattle. The gray imposter had been rubbed with charcoal until it was black, but the charcoal could be washed off if necessary. True, the imposter wasn't the horse that Iron Soldier was, but it was young and strong and it could and would finish the race ahead of the Gunsmith if it had a sizeable lead.

But Max didn't figure to need the imposter. He wanted—

and fully intended—to win this race on one horse. It was just that he was a prudent man, one who believed in leaving nothing to chance; even the most skilled rider and finest horse in the world could make a mistake that would prove disastrous. A single misstep and a leg was broken or, at the least, a hoof was rock-bruised.

"Afternoon!" a young farmer called, appearing from behind his barn. He was soon followed by his pretty, but weary-looking wife. The farmer was carrying a pail of milk and his wife was leading a thin cow. The farmer stopped in his tracks and stared at Max. "Can I help you?"

"I'd like a little grain for my horse and the use of your water," Max said, noting how the farm was in a poor state of repair. The fences were falling down and mended by wire instead of new boards fastened to the posts with nails. There was a broken-down buckboard and the house was sod; it could not have been more than ten by twenty feet in its outside dimensions. Max added, "Of course, I'm willing to pay."

The couple exchanged glances. "Cash money?" the farmer asked, as if that was too much to expect.

"Sure," Max said. "I'll pay you a dollar for a bucket of oats, barley, wheat, or whatever grain you have for my gray horse."

"Well, we do have that much. Have a whole sack of oats left that you could have for another dollar."

"You do?"

The young farmer nodded eagerly.

Max gave the matter a moment of thought. "You seem to be the only sodbusters farming out this way."

"We are."

"All right, then I'll take the sack of oats and if you want to unsaddle my horse and curry him down real good, then I'll pay four bits for that, too."

"I'm sorry," the woman said. "All we have is my hairbrush. Don't have a horse of our own."

"Your hairbrush will do," he said, wondering how much finer the young woman would look in a clean dress with her face scrubbed, her cheeks rouged, and wearing lipstick and a fancy comb in her hair. She'd look good enough to work in a dance hall and have the cowboys standing in line. "I'll pay you another dollar which ought to buy you a new one and leave you change."

"Oh, yes, sir!" the woman exclaimed, running into the house.

When she was out of earshot, Max looked at the young man and said, "This is no place to bring a woman like that, alone and at the mercy of Indians. You ought to buy a race horse like this one and make some money in the city."

"But I can't afford a good horse." The young man was thin and apologetic-sounding. "I can't even afford a bad horse, mister."

"You could if you sold everything you and your wife own. Maybe."

"But what about a place to live!"

"Live in a tent!" Max said impatiently. "When I was your age, I did that and worse in order to save enough money to buy my first race horse. And look at me today! I'm rich. You've heard of Max Holloway and this horse, Iron Soldier, haven't you?"

"I'm sorry, sir. But I'm afraid I have not."

Max was disgusted. "Well, maybe you're just too damned ignorant to make money then."

The farmer's cheeks reddened. "I word hard from sunup to sundown. I'm honest and thrifty. I'll do and so will the missus."

"You'll do nothing out here that will ever put you into the real money," Max said. "And you very well may get yourself and that girl scalped by a party of Sioux warriors. Young man, you're an ignorant fool."

The farmer started to say something in his defense but at that moment, his wife came hurrying out. Her face was all aglow and she held a brush aloft and said, "It was my mother's. But she wouldn't mind if I used it on your horse. She'd understand."

Max nodded and had to look away. This couple was pathetic and as soon as they'd finished brushing Iron Soldier, he'd be moving on. "By the way," he added. "I'll take some of that milk for another four bits."

The young couple looked as if they had found gold. In truth, to a couple of losers like this, five dollars was a hell of a lot of money. Why, he wouldn't have paid them that much for their damn sorry cow.

Max was annoyed that he could not have gotten the woman off by herself for a few minutes. Maybe she was sick of this life and yeared for something better. Maybe she liked the looks of him a whole lot better than her young, down-and-out husband. Max knew he cut quite a handsome figure in his new buckskin outfit. Enough of one to turn a young lady's head and put a sparkle in her eyes.

He said to the woman, "You ever get into Cheyenne?"

Her eyes darted to those of her husband and then she looked back at him. "No, sir. Laramie has all we need."

"Cheyenne has a whole lot more to offer." When the woman kept brushing the gray, Max said, "If you ever get tired of this life, ask for Max Holloway in Cheyenne. I can help."

The young farmer exploded with anger. "Dammit, we don't need your help!"

His fists were balled up at his sides. Max sneered at him. "I'm not interested in helping you, it's your woman that's caught my fancy."

The farmer rushed him and Max coolly stepped to one side and threw out his leg, tripping the younger man to the ground. Then, before he could recover, Max drove the toe of his boot into the man's belly and doubled him up, gagging in pain.

"You're no gentleman!" the young woman cried. "Get off our farm."

Max chuckled. He took five dollars out of his wallet and threw it at them. "You ever wise up and want a *real* man to hold you at night, you get yourself washed up and come to Cheyenne. Hear me?"

The woman looked up at him with tears in her eyes. "Just git!"

Max checked his cinch and hoisted the sack of oats over his saddle. Then, with his pocket knife, he stabbed a three-inch gash in the sack and led his horse west.

The farmer and his wife stared and then the young man could not help but yell, "If'n you was going to let it spill, why'd you pay for it, mister? If you want to put my grain to waste, then cross my fields, dammit!"

Max grinned because he could hear the frustration and the anger in the young sodbuster's voice. But he didn't stop walking the gray until the sack had run itself out. It was the last grain for miles around and when the Gunsmith finally passed this way, he was going to have to feed his horse prairie grass.

NINE

Duke went lame at the very crest of the Laramie Mountains. One minute he was going along like a trooper, the next he was favoring his right foreleg. Clint was out of the saddle and beside the animal in a moment. He picked up the gelding's right foot, hoping that there was nothing more than a rock jammed between the iron shoe and horse's soft frog. But to his surprise, the shoe was missing.

Clint swore in anger. Why, he'd had the black gelding shod only a few days earlier and he'd personally overseen the job to make sure it was done right. Now, in the darkness, he struck a match and held it close to the hoof. Careful examination showed that the hoof had been tampered with. If the shoe had simply fallen off, some of the nails would still have been protruding from the hoof wall. But in this case it was obvious that someone had pulled out all the hoof nails except two or three. On the flatlands west of Cheyenne, the shoe had managed to stay tacked in place but on a rocky mountainside, the stress of hitting so many rocks had knocked the shoe free.

"Holloway," Clint gritted between clenched teeth, "I'll get you for this!"

The Gunsmith looked up at the stars and debated his sorry predicament. He could lead the gelding on down the mountainside and be in Laramie City by late afternoon, or he could backtrack and hope to find the lost shoe. He had some horseshoe nails and could tack the shoe on with the butt of his gun. He'd done it many times before. But what if the shoe had fallen off miles back? In that case, he might waste hours searching and moving in the wrong direction only to miss it in the darkness.

Clint looked up at the stars and calculated it was almost five o'clock in the morning. It would be daylight soon.

"I'll give it two hours," he muttered, turning the gelding around and heading back east.

He saw the lost horseshoe right at daybreak when the eastern skylight was the color of melting butter. Clint picked the shoe up and quickly tacked it back on. Satisfied, he wearily climbed back into the saddle and retraced his steps west again. He had not had any sleep in two nights and he was dead tired. He remembered that Max Holloway had a special harness or some such damn thing made to hold him erect in the saddle while Iron Soldier moved along.

Clint had no such device. He just dropped his chin down on his chest and catnapped, sometimes coming awake when Duke stepped over a fallen log or slipped on a stretch of unstable shale. But he slept, just as he had slept many times before when trailing a fugitive of the law whom he was determined to track down and bring to justice. It was not a good, restful sleep, but it could keep a man going night after night in the saddle and give him enough rest to keep alert and on his guard.

Miles west of Laramie City, he came to the same farm that Max Holloway had passed through early that morning.

"What do you want, mister?" the young sodbuster de-

WINNER TAKE ALL 65

manded, stepping out of his house with a shotgun clenched in his fists.

Clint caught a glimpse of a young woman behind him. She was pretty, but weary-looking and marked by the anxiety on her face. She was probably no more than seventeen, but she appeared to be five or six years older. Hard work, loneliness, and poverty aged women almost as much as too much sun and too many children.

"I'd like some water from your well and some grain for my horse."

"Water will cost you two bits. Don't have anymore grain. A man on a gray stallion come through and bought the only sack we had. Then he spilled it on his way out, so the chickens ate it all."

"That sounds like Max Holloway, all right," Clint said, dismounting stiffly and easing an oaken bucket down a rope into the little well. He heard it splash about ten feet below and when he hauled it up, the water was brackish and had a poor taste.

"It tastes better in the springtime," the sodbuster said. "If your horse won't drink it, you can drink your fill for a dime."

Clint looked around at the place. "How come you settled clear out here by yourselves? Nothing but a train coming along once or twice a week. Must get pretty lonesome with Laramie City so far away."

A lot of people must have asked him the same question because he bristled slightly and had a pat answer. "Someday, there will be farms aplenty all over this valley. I mean to be the first and to stake some of this land for ourselves. In ten, twenty years, I'll be a wealthy man. Maybe get a town named after me."

Clint let Duke drink his fill. "You won't be able to last

that long out here," he said. "This country will starve you out. It's too high and too cold for crops. If you're a farmer, you ought to go to California or Oregon. Mild winters, good grass and soil. You'd do a whole lot better there."

"We think different." The sodbuster studied Clint nervously. "You're gonna pay us for that water, ain't ya?"

Clint looked at the young woman. He tried not to think about what easy prey these people would be for Indians. "Yeah," he said, digging the change out of his pocket and tossing it to the man who had to drop his shotgun and make a grab for the money.

Clint remounted his horse and said, "How long ago did the man on the gray stallion come through?"

"About eight hours ago. Why, you chasing him for some reason?"

"I don't have time to explain. I sure wish you and that young wife of yours would go to California or Oregon. You're easy game for the Indians and this is poor farming country."

"That's what the other man said before he kicked me in the gut," the sodbuster snarled. "I'll thank you to get off our farm now."

Clint rode away and he never looked back. An eight-hour headstart was not insurmountable at this early stage of the race, but it was something to worry about. Iron Soldier was a hell of a fine animal and in top condition. It was going to take some doing to overtake him before they reached Salt Lake City.

Clint touched the spurs to Duke and let the animal settle into a long, ground-eating stride that the black gelding could sustain for hours. To keep from fretting about the awful start he had gotten off to, he thought about Vicki Flowers. Thought about how she felt in his arms and when she kissed him. He could hear the sound of her laughter and almost

WINNER TAKE ALL

smell her perfume and the taste of wine on her lips. The Union Pacific train which she and Shorty were riding was a long way ahead of him now. He'd bet anything that Vicki was worried sick about him and Duke. He'd catch them in a few days, but until then, there was just no way that he could get word to her that he was still in a horse race and still confident that he could win. Vicki would just have to keep the faith.

When the Union Pacific train had pulled into Medicine Bow, Vicki Flowers did not even get off at the station to stretch her legs. She had been trying to forget that the Gunsmith was far, far behind and probably already out of the running. It was *so* depressing. She had been sure that the black gelding was the better of the two horses and that Clint would somehow figure out a way to win. But now . . . now even Shorty looked glum and inconsolable.

Vicki had been sitting alone in the dining car when a very handsome man in his thirties had asked to join her. Ordinarily, she would have declined his company but he seemd so vigorous and confident and she felt so low and dispirited that she thought his company might cheer her.

Now, as the hours passed and the train rolled through Carbon Station, then Benton, and was heading for Rawlings, she was delighted to have made his acquaintance. He was a little too brash and prone to brag, but he was nice and his attentions cheered her considerably.

"So," he said, "you see how difficult it is for me. When you inherit a huge newspaper that has been in the family for three generations, there's an immense amount of pressure to do better than your forefathers. I was the head of my class at Yale and could have pursued any field I chose, but I chose to accept the challenge of carrying on the family tradition, the great *Bouchard* tradition."

"How very courageous of you," she told him, "Ummm, how much is the newspaper worth?"

He leaned forward and grinned lasciviously. "What you really want to know, beautiful Miss Flowers, is how much am *I* worth."

Vicki laughed a little too loudly. "Yes," she said, sipping her drink. "I suppose that is exactly what I was wondering."

"I'm worth more money than you can even imagine," he said with a wink that indicated that the rich young publisher's drinks were taking their effect.

"Oh, I can imagine a lot of money."

"Try a million dollars," he said straight-faced.

The drink almost fell out of her hand. "A million dollars!"

"That's what I could sell my stock for tomorrow. Easy."

"Whew! I never knew anyone that rich." It was true. Compared to this man, even Max Holloway was a pauper. And Bobby Bouchard wasn't married and would be a whole lot more manageable than Max had ever been.

"What about you?" he asked, letting his eyes drift to her large bosom. "The word I hear is that you and the famous Gunsmith . . . well, that's why everyone is staying away from you. Who'd be crazy enough to fool around with a professional gunfighter's woman?"

"I don't know," she said, "but I'm not his woman. We are . . . well . . . good friends. I wanted him to win this race."

"Why? The other man has everything going for him. I heard about this thing as I was already planning to go to Virginia City to meet a fellow named Sam Clemens. He's good and I'm going to hire him for my paper. Besides, when I heard about this race, I thought it would be fun. I'm a fine writer, you know. If I wasn't so busy with running the paper, I'd enjoy doing the same kinds of things that Mark Twain is writing for the *Territorial Enterprise*. In

WINNER TAKE ALL

fact, I could teach him a few things that might even make him a lot of money and get his name wider notice."

"I've never heard of him," she said.

"Not too many people have east of the Rockies. But having a genius for writing, I can recognize it when I see it in others. Twain has talent. Real talent. I pay well for *all* kinds of talents, Miss Flowers. Especially when I am traveling alone."

Again, his glance dropped to her bosom and this time, it lingered there. So, Vicki thought, he is going to proposition me with money for a few nights in his sleeper coach. No thanks. Why settle for peanuts and beer when you can have lobster and champagne?

"Ahh, Miss Flowers. I was wondering if you might enjoy a visit to my private coach? It's really quite nice and I have something to show you."

"Yes," she said. "I'll just bet you do." Vicki stood up and patted his cheek. "Thank you, but no thank you."

He was astonished at her reply. She saw his face reflect shock and Vicki guessed that handsome young bachelors worth a million dollars did not often face rejection.

"But we are getting along so beautifully and the night is young!" His voice was imploring. "I'd assumed . . . I mean, I'd hoped. . . . "

"You hoped we could meet for breakfast," she said sweetly. "And that would be delightful. Now, good-night."

Vicki walked away, feeling eyes ravaging her swaying figure. Let him suffer with anticipation. She would build him up to a fever pitch and then pick him clean, for though they were probably about the same age, he was a boy. Max Holloway was a man, a hard, calculating, and difficult man. Clint Adams was a man, too. A dizzying lover and a real gentleman despite his reputation. But Bobby Bouchard was still a boy. Probably a very experienced boy with girls, but totally out of his league with real women who would eat him alive.

And maybe I will eat him, she thought with a cattish smile. Maybe I will become a millionairess if I choose.

Vicki went back to her second-class coach, which was filled with reporters and cigar smoke. Shorty Evans was traveling third class and sleeping on a wooden bench if he slept at all.

Vicki settled down in her seat and closed her eyes. The end of another day in the race and Clint Adams was miles and miles behind.

How depressing. If only dear Clint had Bobby Bouchard's mountain of money. What a pair they would make!

TEN

Clint pushed Duke hard and when he passed through Benton, he learned that he had cut Holloway's lead time by two hours. The Gunsmith felt sure that he could make up the distance over the next two weeks it would take them to reach Carson City. If he could just whittle down Holloway's lead by an hour a day he would be fine. That evening, Clint distanced himself a mile from the railroad tracks and found a small meadow. He unsaddled the gelding and let him graze for three hours while he slept. At midnight, he resaddled feeling much better. Sleeping on horseback was fine for catnapping, and a man could do it for quite some time, but it left him jangled and jumpy. Clint also knew that Duke needed to graze. Holloway might think he could get by with feeding Iron Soldier nothing but grain, but that would not work too long. A horse needed hay or grass, too, otherwise it got colicky and got sick.

Dawn found Clint west of Rawlings, following the tracks which had become as much part of the prairie as the grass and the sky. He crossed over the Continental Divide but there was nothing special about it. It was high desert country that he dropped down into. Great Basin country covered with stunted sagebrush, some alkali flats, and lots of runty tufts of prairie grass. He saw hundreds of antelope, but no buffalo. They were almost gone from the face of the frontier now. The transcontinental railroad had severed their north/south migration route, and buffalo hunters and even railroad train passengers had all but wiped them out. There might be a few left in some hidden valleys or canyons, and maybe even more than that had drifted up into Canada's cold country where few whites dared to venture, but they were sure gone in this neck of the woods.

This southern Wyoming was lonesome and empty except for the railroad tracks he followed. Not that Clint was complaining. The last thing he wanted to see was Indians and this was still Sioux and Crow hunting territory but a man did yearn for company after a time. For two days he rode without seeing a single person and his eyes were filled with long vistas, broken bluffs, and a vast, sweeping country that seemed to roll on and on. The colors were magnificent in the Red Desert but mostly, Clint's eyes were fixed straight ahead. He had fallen into a routine of stopping at each railroad town and heading for the livery where he would put Duke up for four hours with all the hay he wanted and a bucket of grain for dessert. While Duke ate, Clint napped in the stall next to him on a bed of straw. He would awake feeling much better and then he would go on.

At each stop, he would be greeted by well-wishers and learn how far he was behind Holloway and the special train that was staying with the leader. Clint was gaining on Iron Soldier. Not nearly as much or as fast as he'd hoped, but that just meant that Holloway was pushing his horse too fast. Clint knew that, sooner or later, even as gallant an animal as Iron Soldier would break down under the pace that Holloway was riding.

It was just a matter of time.

WINNER TAKE ALL

* * *

Max was furious as he paced back and forth at the Rock Springs Livery. "What the hell is wrong with my horse!" he shouted. "Doc, I'm paying you a fortune to do nothing but keep Iron Soldier in good health and now you say he'd got the colic! Make him well!"

The veterinarian threw up his hands with exasperation. "What you don't seem to understand is that this horse—any horse—has to have time to eat hay or grass."

"If he has all the grain he wants, what does he need hay or grass for? We haven't got time for him to eat grass. He could eat grass or hay for eight hours a day."

"That's right," the veterinarian said. "The theory is that hay is fibrous enough to stimulate the stomach's walls and help digestion. With just grain, it won't work."

"Jesus!" Max swore. "I never heard of such a thing!"

"I have," the veterinarian said. "But grain poisoning is rare. I mean, why would anyone feed expensive grain exclusive of cheaper, probably equally nutritious hay?"

"Why? to win a thousand-mile horse race, that's why!"

The veterinarian was a large man with a red face and little glasses. He looked scholarly and was. Son of an Illinois horse breeder, he had been raised with horses and he knew he was right. "You hired me to tell you how to keep Iron Soldier going. I've kept his legs sound and now, I'm telling you he will recover completely if you allow the horse to rest and eat hay until tomorrow."

"I'll give him twelve hours," Max growled. "You better have him ready to run. If I lose this race, that's ten thousand dollars plus twice that in side bets that's gone. I'll make sure you regret the loss as much as I, Doc."

The veterinarian said, "Let's see how he feels in twelve hours. Get some sleep, Mr. Holloway. You need the rest almost as much as he does. That custom-made harness you had designed to keep you from falling out of the saddle is a hazard. Go back to your private coach on the train and sleep. We'll wake you in time. I promise I'll stay right here with Iron Soldier. But you have to realize, you're pushing yourself and this horse way too hard."

"I pushed a lot harder when I rode the Pony Express."

"Yes, and you were twenty years younger and had a string of horses to ride. This is different. The man who wins is the one who will pace himself and his horse. You *have* to slow down."

"I'll slow down in my grave." Holloway barked to his men, "Spike, you, Ed and Jess come with me and keep those reporters off my back. The rest of you, guard this door and don't let them damned nosy sonofabitches come inside."

The moment he stepped outside, he was mobbed by a pack of anxious reporters. "Gerald Dana from the *Boston Globe*. Is it true that Iron Soldier is down and dying."

"Hell, no!"

"But we saw the horse and that veterinarian, Doc Potter. It looked grim."

Max shook his head. "That's not true. Iron Soldier is fit and ready to go on. I've just decided to rest him for twelve hours."

"Twelve hours!" another reporter exclaimed. "Why, we got a telegram from the Bitter Creek railroad station just now saying that the Gunsmith is passing through. That's less than fifty miles from here. The Gunsmith will pass you in twelve hours."

"No he won't," Max said. "His horse will need to rest, too."

"Not no twelve hours, he won't."

Max had to curb his outburst of temper. "I never claimed

WINNER TAKE ALL

this race would be easy for either one of us. But I'm still far in the lead and I'll stay in the lead."

"Not with a colicky horse," a reporter said. "If Iron Soldier is in trouble, you owe it to us to say so right now."

"He isn't in trouble, you pin-headed sonofabitch!" Max shouted, knocking the man aside.

The reporter was shaken, but he headed directly for the telegraph office, with several of his peers hot on his tail. "You going to tell the world that the great Max Holloway damn near knocked you down!"

"You bet I am," the reporter snapped. "But even more important, I'm going to tell the world that Holloway and the Iron Soldier are in trouble. And from the sound of Holloway, it's serious. I think that his horse might even be dying."

The flock of reporters stampeded away.

Max went into conference with Spike, Ed, and Jess. "Listen," he told them. "No matter what happens, Iron Soldier and I have to stay out front. I took the lead out of Cheyenne and I don't want to be passed. Spike, you, Ed, and Jess are going to slow the Gunsmith down."

The three gunmen exchanged glances. Spike was their leader, a dark, taciturn man with a hard reputation. "You want us to stop him, or just slow him?"

"Slow him, I said! Don't kill him or his horse. It's too early for anything so drastic. I just don't want him to ride out of here before our horse is fit to run. That's all."

"Boss," Spike protested, "he's gonna keep coming unless he's dead! You know that as well as I do. Let us just put a bullet into him. We can take his body and shove his boot through his stirrup and let that horse drag him until there ain't nothing to recognize."

"And what about the bullet in his body?"

"I'll dig it out if I can't put it through his throat," Spike said.

But Max shook his head. "If you do that, all those damned newspaper reporters will smell a rat. They'll guess we had the man killed and even if it can't be proved, it would tarnish my reputation. I want to beat the Gunsmith to Carson City, not have him shot before we get to Nevada. If he's close to me when we reach Elko, Nevada, then we may have to take more drastic measures."

Spike was not pleased. He knew the Gunsmith was not a man to tinker or play pitty-pat with. If you got fancy and tried to wing him, or get close enough to get the drop on him altogether, he was still going to cause you trouble. "I'll figure out some way to delay the man."

"Good. Make it a *long* delay."

"I will, but don't forget you still have Gray Man."

Gray Man was Max's ringer horse. Max nodded his head. "Yeah, I know. But let's see if we can do this without him. Either way, I mean to win. Now get out of here, all of you, except Spike."

When he and Spike were alone, Max said, "Tell me about Vicki. What's she doing on the train? Has she quit the Gunsmith yet?"

"I don't know," Spike said, choosing his words carefully. "But I got a feeling she has. She's spending a lot of time in the fancy dining car with some rich eastern publisher."

"What!"

"It's true," Spike said. "Now, there may not be anything to it. His name is Bobby Bouchard. I hear he's richer than you, even. At any rate, it seems he'd taken quite a fancy to Vicki."

"Damn!" Max shouted in a fit of jealousy. "There I am, looking like a national hero and gloriously riding my ass

WINNER TAKE ALL

off while she's fucking some rich newspaper man! I'll kill her!"

Spike raised his hand. "I don't think she's fucking anyone," he said. "She's sleeping in the second-class coach along with most of the reporters."

"Then why. . ."

"I just wanted you to know," Spike said, already sorry he'd mentioned this complication. He knew that Max still considered his ex-wife as personal property and one of the most important reasons for winning this race was to prove to Vicki that he was a better man than the Gunsmith.

"Well, if she isn't sleeping with the bastard yet, she will be by the time we reach Nevada, if he's ticketed that far."

"He is. I checked," Spike said. "He's ticketed to Reno."

"You watch her!" Max said, his voice stretched with anger and fatigue. "If he takes her to bed, I'll have you boys fix him for keeps."

Spike nodded. "I just think we'd best worry about the Gunsmith first."

Max poured himself a stiff drink and swallowed it in quick gulps before he collapsed on his narrow sleeping compartment bed and closed his eyes. "Spike?"

"Yeah?"

"Don't tell anyone, but this race is hard. A hell of a lot harder than riding for the Pony Express. Every muscle and joint in my body is aching. The goddamn sleep harness doesn't work worth a damn, and now Iron Soldier is even causing me worry."

"Just sleep and let me and the boys think of some way to delay the Gunsmith. With him held up a day or so, you'll rest easier."

"Yeah," Max said, closing his eyes and feeling the liquor warm his belly. "You're right. Before this is over, you might just have to earn your money this month."

Spike stopped at the door and turned back to the exhausted man he worked for. "Just remember that you promised me and the boys half of your winnings."

Max's eyes popped open. "The deal was a third!"

"Yeah, but that was before you decided we set out to 'delay' Clint Adams. That makes it a whole lot riskier. I think it deserves a lot more than a third."

Max stared at the lean, deadly gunfighter. He was not afraid of Spike Dalton, but neither did he like the idea of crossing the man over a few thousand dollars. Spike had him right now but there would come a day—a faster gun for hire—and then this would be remembered. "All right, half."

Spike tipped his Stetson. "Thanks, boss. I knew you'd appreciate the spot you've just put us in."

"Don't fail!"

Spike grinned and then he was gone.

ELEVEN

Salt Wells was as desolate a little whistle stop as there was on the entire transcontinental railroad. Except for the train station, a surprisingly plush saloon, and a dry goods store that also sold guns and ammunition, there was nothing that would hold a man, except Margarita Montoya. Everyone who saw her wondered why she was living in such a northern climate and in such a desolate place as this. Why, with her flashing eyes, pearly teeth, and voluptuous figure, she could have made a fortune along any of the towns along the Mexican border.

In truth, she was making a fortune at Salt Wells. Margarita owned the saloon in partnership with a giant named Beltran who treated her with the respect of a nun and would kill or maim any man who did not do the same. Beltran worshipped Margarita and bought her presents and even tried to raise roses behind his shack to make her happy.

Margarita *was* happy, or at least satisfied. Raised the daughter of a vaquero who had driven cattle up from Mexico only to get shot in Wyoming, Margarita had remained until she had amassed a good deal of money and bought into her own saloon. And though she could have gone back to Mexico, she did not. Wyoming had become a part of her, though she could not abide its winters and had recently taken to going south to Arizona Territory where she would spend several months basking in the warmth of Tucson.

In Tucson, it was thought that she was the daughter of a rich and powerful rancher. She was treated with great respect and it carried over when she returned in the springtime to Wyoming. Her return always generated a grand celebration by men who had saved their winter wages in order to spend a few hours with Margarita. For there was little doubt that she was the prettiest whore in Wyoming. Her lovemaking was legendary; passengers on the Union Pacific were known to miss their train in order to experience her embrace, if only for a few frenetic minutes.

A few men were favored enough to intimately know the señorita free of charge, but their numbers she could count on both hands. Many more paid an outrageous sum to make love to her, and even more were denied that pleasure and honor at any price. Margarita was selective and refused to share an embrace with any man who was drunk, dirty, or coarse. A refused man would often feel insulted and grow angry and abusive. In that case, Beltran would beat him half to death, tie his broken body across his horse or throw it into his wagon, and then send the man away. A very few returned to kill Beltran, and they always learned at the moment of their death a very important fact—both Beltran and the señorita were experts with a gun.

Spike was one of the few men that had been rejected by Margarita and then returned years later to finally know the señorita as a man does a woman. At sixteen, he had fallen in love with the señorita, but had been spurned as being too young. He'd flown into a rage and actually grabbed the lovely señorita. But then, seeing her giant coming to kill him, he'd had the good sense to fall to his knees and present her with a flower just as Beltran was about to blow the top of his head off with his Army Colt.

WINNER TAKE ALL   81

When the train with its reporters had passed through Salt Wells the day before, Spike had wanted to see Margarita, but she had been "entertaining" Bobby Bouchard, who had, somehow, also heard of her loveliness. Spike had been angry, but philisophical enough to know that Margarita had probably taken the wealthy man for several hundred dollars. Unfortunately, there had been no time to see Margarita, for the train had stopped only long enough to take on water.

Now, however, as he, Jess, and Ed galloped hard into Salt Wells station and tied their horses up before Margarita's saloon, Spike did not have the luxury of reacquainting himself with Margarita. Instead, he was seeking Beltran. He found the giant tending bar and after a cordial but unenthusaistic greeting, he took Beltran aside.

"I have bad news," he said to the giant. "There is a man, a very famous gunman who is coming along any minute. He means to have Miss Montoya and then kill her for her money."

Beltran's eyes narrowed. He had a low forehead and he spoke slowly, for he was not particularly bright. "Why should he do this?"

"He was refused by her many years ago. He has changed in ways that make it seem as if he is a stranger. But he is not! In fact, there is none more deadly. You must hurt him."

"I will kill him."

"No!" Spike took a deep breath. "He is too famous. His death would raise many questions. Do as you have done with the others, beat him and then tie him across his horse and send him away. If he comes back again, *then* kill him."

Beltran nodded. He had immense overhanging brows and a jaw made of granite. His chest was bigger around than a pickle barrel and arms were larger than any blacksmith's that Spike had ever seen. "You are sure?"

"Yes," Spike said. "He will be here soon. He is very,

very good with a gun. Do not give him a chance to show you. Understand?"

Spike started toward the back room where Margarita lived and entertained her male guests. "No," Beltran said.

Spike halted in his tracks. He looked down the bar at Jess and Ed who could kill Beltran at his signal. "What do you mean 'no'?" he asked.

"She is busy."

"Dammit! She was busy when the train came through, who is it this time?"

Beltran shrugged. He did not like to think too much about the men that Margarita saw and was happiest when they were alone for days at a stretch without any visitors.

The sound of approaching hoofbeats marked the Gunsmith's arrival. Spike moved to hide behind a curtain near the old piano and yelled, "Jess, Ed, stay out of it unless you're needed."

The two men poured more whiskey. Spike had told them what to expect with Beltran, but the background had not prepared them for the size of the giant. It seemed impossible that Beltran could also have speed in his hands but they were not willing to test their doubts. Both men were plenty content to sit back and wait to see what happened next. If the giant failed to hurt the Gunsmith, they would do whatever it took to put him temporarily out of commission.

Clint tied Duke to the hitching rail outside of the saloon and dry goods store. He was running low on jerked beef and thinking he might enjoy some dried peaches to chew on while he traveled. But most of all, he wanted grain for Duke.

"Hello, there," he said to the giant who glowered at him. "I need a few supplies. But first, how long ago did the westbound train pass this way?"

WINNER TAKE ALL 83

Beltran glared at him so fiercely that Clint grew a little uneasy. "I'm in a horse race," Clint added, making another stab at being friendly. "I know the train came through and the last I heard, it was about five hours ahead of me. Is that true?"

Again, the giant showed no sign of outward comprehension.

"What's the matter with you?" Clint asked. "Did I say something wrong when I walked in or are you a mute?"

In answer, the giant reached across the counter and grabbed Clint by the collar and lifted him completely off his feet, then slammed his forehead against Clint's, almost knocking him out cold.

The Gunsmith tried to grab for his Colt, but he was dazed and the gun clattered uselessly to the dirt floor of the saloon. Then the man was dragging him over the counter and onto the narrow aisle behind it. A huge fist was raised overhead and Clint rolled his head sideways. The fist caught him against the side of the temple and lights exploded behind his eyes. He stabbed upward with stiff fingers and was lucky enought to find an eye socket.

The giant howled in pain and Clint used that moment to strike for the man's exposed throat. It was a weak blow, but it did manage to choke the giant for an instant and by the time he caught his breath, Clint was dragging himself to his feet. The giant lurched forward and the Gunsmith buried his fist in the man's gut but it was like striking a pile of buffalo hides. There was a little give, but not much. Clint shot a jab into the man's nose and heard it crack. But he took a booming overhand right that sent him backpeddling down the aisle.

The mad giant was after him like a cat on a mouse. He grabbed Clint and hurled him across the room, knocking over shelves laden with blankets. The Gunsmith ducked another haymaker and ripped his knee up into the giant's testicles. Beltran howled and grabbed for his crotch and Clint hit him flush on the jaw with a stiff left jab. It was a mistake. The man's jaw was like rock and Clint pulled his fist away certain that he had broken or at least dislocated a knuckle. The giant rocked back on his heels and Clint grabbed a new pick handle from the floor and raised it.

Clint did not want to use the pick handle. He was afraid he'd have to whack the giant so hard he might even kill him. Glancing over at Jess and Ed, he shouted, "Hey! You men down there! What the hell is wrong with this crazy man! Tell him to back off or I'll split his head wide open."

The two men didn't say a word and the giant charged. Clint had no choice but to use the handle. He timed his swing perfectly and it flashed downward. The giant raised a forearm to block the strike but the handle was coming in too fast and he could not protect his head. When the handle struck the man's skull, he dropped like a stone and lay still.

Clint's chest was heaving, his ears were ringing, and he was furious. "Why didn't you two sonofabitches warn me he was out of his mind!"

They turned away from the bar and started to go for their guns.

Clint could not believe what was happening! He dove behind the counter and clawed for his fallen six-gun. When it was in his grasp, he rolled as two bullets bit into the sawdust. Then, the Gunsmith's six-shooter was bucking in his fist and the pair were backpeddling, their arms rotating like those of a Kansas windmill.

Before he could raise to his feet, Clint felt danger from behind and tried to twist around in time to defend himself. There wasn't time. A blinding pain filled his skull and dropped him spinning into a fissure of darkness.

• • •

WINNER TAKE ALL

Margarita Montoya came racing out of her room to see Spike standing over a fallen man with a pick handle in his fists. She glanced over and saw two dead men, and then she saw Beltran lying facedown. Margarita ran to him and fell at his side. She rolled the giant over on his back and her finger's flew to the pulse at his throat. He was alive but unconscious.

"What happened, Señor Spike!"

Spike ignored her question. "Who's in your room?"

"No one! I was taking a siesta."

Spike didn't believe her. He looked into the room. The bed was rumpled but not unmade. The room was empty.

"What happened?" she cried.

Spike came back out and said, pointing to Clint, "That man wouldn't leave without having you. Beltran tried to stop him. Then the others. Finally, I have managed to get him."

Margarita stood up. "The two dead hombres were your friends?"

"No. I met them just now."

"Will you bury them?"

"No." Spike reached for the señorita and pulled her to himself. "I didn't think you'd remember me after all these years."

"Of course I do. You've changed."

"So has Beltran. He's never failed before. Maybe he's getting too old to take care of you any longer."

"Let go of me!"

"Not a chance. You taught a boy everything he knew about making love," Spike said. "I didn't even realize it then, but it was true. Now, I'm a man and I've come back to see if you've learned any new tricks."

"I should have let Beltran kill you the last time," she hissed. "I showed you mercy, and this is what I get for it."

"Yeah," he growled, dragging her into her room and throwing her on the bed. "It is!"

He grabbed the front of her dress and tore it down to her belly, revealing her large, cinnamon-brown breasts. "I never forgot the first time I tasted these," he panted, burying his face between them as she struggled to fight him off.

Spike had not felt such urgency to make love to a woman since the last time he had held her. He let go of her wrists and jerked her dress up over her hips then fumbled with his pant's buttons.

Too late, he heard the sound of the derringer's hammer cock back. He looked up to see her with the pistol in her fist. "You forgot that I keep this under my pillow," she said.

With his right hand still digging for his manhood, he used his left to grab for the derringer, and when it exploded, its .44 bullet went right through the palm of his hand and entered his skull just below his left eye socket. Spike slapped his face and rolled off the bed. He was dead before he hit the floor, with his gunhand still trapped inside his fly.

Margarita climbed unsteadily from the bed. She walked over to the mirror and sat down at her makeup table and selected a brush. Expressionless, she brushed her hair until it was perfect. Her heart slowed and only once did she look down at the dead man and then she spat on him.

"You were one of the very few that I spared out of mercy, and look what it has cost me. Three, maybe four men for Beltran to bury."

When she was finished combing her hair and composing herself, she lifted her chin and went out to care for Beltran, who was still out cold. His head was badly cut and she bathed the scalp wound in cool water until the giant's eyes fluttered open.

Satisfied that he would be all right, Margarita went over to see the Gunsmith. When she touched the pulse at his throat and realized that he was still alive, her first impulse was to kill him before he awakened. But then she reasoned that, if he had been Señor Spike's enemy, perhaps he was not a bad man after all. So she tied his hands behind his back and then his ankles. She would decide later if he was to live or to die.

She emptied the Gunsmith's pockets, then fleeced the pockets of the other three dead men and was pleased to take almost two hundred dollars. Even after she hired someone to bury the dead, there would be a nice profit.

Margarita went back to her room and smoothed the comforter on her bed. She had almost been raped and the experience was not to her liking. Perhaps Spike had been right and Beltran was getting old.

Margarita returned to her saloon and poured herself a stiff drink before settling into her favorite chair by the front window. She watched Beltran regain consciousness and she wondered about the man she had tied hand and foot. He was handsome and had the cut of a gambler about him. Certainly, he was no ordinary cowboy. The señorita liked mysterious men. So few were mysterious, and she hoped this one had an interesting story to tell her.

She lit a Mexican cigarillo and waited, confident that within the hour, she would have all the answers.

TWELVE

Clint awoke slowly, his head feeling as if it had been split wide open by the open blade of an ax. He groaned, opened his eyes, and saw a pair of the largest boots he had ever seen in his life. Suddenly, a pair of hands attached themselves to his shirt and he was dragged off the floor and slammed into a chair. Only then did he realize that he was bound hand and foot.

"Señor, who are you?" a woman's voice asked.

Clint raised his head and his eyes met those of a beautiful Mexican woman. "What happened? Where am I?"

"You are at Margarita Montoya's saloon in Salt Wells," she informed him. "Here, drink this and it will help."

She held a glass of whiskey to his lips. He drank, anxious to try anything to ease the pain that radiated out from the base of his skull. The whiskey burned his throat and almost immediately a warmth spread to his limbs. "More," he grunted.

He finished the glass and felt the pain begin to subside. "Why am I tied up?"

"Because you killed three men," the señorita said with a smile, as if it were a little joke they shared. "And because we do not have a sheriff and so you will have to be taken

WINNER TAKE ALL

to Cheyenne. Perhaps there is a reward on you, eh?"

"Cheyenne? Reward! There's no reward and I've got to get to Nevada."

"Why is that so?"

Clint told her who he was and ended by saying, "This race is big news. Even now, as I sit here tied to your chair, I'm falling farther and farther behind."

Beltran shook his head. "Spike said you was a gunfighter. He said you were dangerous."

"Who's Spike?"

Margarita and the giant exchanged glances. "I think he is telling us the truth, but we can't take the chance. We will hold him until the next train comes through. Perhaps then, we can learn the truth."

"But I *am* telling you the truth!" Clint struggled with helpless fury until the giant doubled up his fists. At that point, the Gunsmith relaxed. "Listen," he said. "There must be a telegraph at the train station. Wire ahead and they'll tell you that I'm the one that is racing Max Holloway to Carson City."

"The telegraph operators always quit after a few weeks," Beltran said. "There is no one."

Clint looked up into the giant's face. He saw the heavy, resolute features indicating dullness and he turned to the señorita. "Listen," he said. "You must have heard the talk about the race. The train couldn't have come through here more than five or six hours ago. Didn't it even stop?"

Margarita thought about the last train through with a smile. Bobby Bouchard had just come into her saloon for a quick drink, but when he had seen her face and figure, he'd forgot about his drink in a hurry. She's seen at once that he was wealthy and when he'd whispered in her ear that he wanted to see her alone, Margarita had quickly obliged him. Taking a chance, she'd asked for a hundred dollars for her favors and he'd paid her so quickly she realized he'd have paid her double that amount. She had tried to make him miss the train, but he'd been in a hurry and taken her very fast. She remembered that he had told her about this insane horse race.

"You are one of the racers?"

"That's right. And I need to get out of here!"

"How do I know this is to be true, señor?"

"You just have to take my word for it."

"That is not good enough. Where is your horse?"

"Tied right outside. He'd the black gelding with the blaze on his face. If you know anything about horses, you'll see in a minute that he'd got speed and endurance."

Margarita walked over to the door and stepped outside. She saw the black gelding tied to a hitch rack and she moved over to study it closely. Duke was sweaty and in need of brushing but that did not hide the fact that he was long-legged and deep of chest. He was a fine-looking animal. Margarita opened Clint's saddlebags and pulled out their contents. There was nothing unusual except for a Cheyenne newspaper that he had used to wrap some jerked beef. She unfolded the paper and there, right on the front page, were headlines proclaiming the big race and then an article describing the two competitors and their horses. By the time that Margarita had finished reading the article, she knew that Clint Adams was also called, "the Gunsmith" and that he had been telling the truth.

For a moment, she weighed the situation, vainly searching for some means to extract more money out of it. She could find none. If Clint were the richer competitor, instead of Max Holloway, and if he were leading the race instead of being so far behind, then there might be some method of parlaying the situation into a nice big profit. But since the article clearly indicated that the Gunsmith was badly under-

WINNER TAKE ALL

financed and a decided underdog, there was nothing to be gained.

"Turn him loose," she said, walking back into the saloon.

Beltran was not pleased with her decision. "But if I do that—"

"Do as I say!"

The giant's eyes sparked with anger, then he nodded. He removed the bonds from Clint's ankles and wrists.

The Gunsmith came unsteadily to his feet. "Is there any grain to be bought here?"

"No," the señorita told him.

"How long was I unconscious?"

"Two, maybe three hours."

Clint shook his throbbing head. "That means that Max Holloway had gained back all the lead time that I've managed to whittle down the last forty-eight hours."

"Would you like another drink? Perhaps something to distract you from this bad news?"

Clint looked into the señorita's dark eyes and managed to shake his head. "Maybe next time."

She pouted. "But why go on if you cannot win?"

"Because a lot can happen between here and Carson City. The race is still not half over. But right now, I'd like my gun back," he said.

"Give it to him," she told the giant.

"But he may kill us!"

"No," she said, "he will not. Give him the gun."

Clint took his weapon, which looked like a toy in the giant's fist. He stumbled outside and the bright light sent new shafts of pain through is skull.

"*Adios*, señor!" Margarita Montoya called. "Remember, on your way back, plan to stay with me longer. You will not regret the delay."

"I'm sure I wouldn't," he told her, crawling onto Duke

and riding west. The sun was plunging toward the western horizon. Clint tried to think of the next town up ahead. He knew that Duke needed grain and rest, but that would have to wait a while longer.

As it was, he could not imagine where he could make up all the time he was already behind.

THIRTEEN

Clint could not believe his eyes when he saw the race's special Union Pacific train waiting at the Rock Springs station. Why wasn't it with Max Holloway on its way to Salt Lake City! He slowed Duke to a trot. Despite the fact that he had slept for several hours during the night and allowed Duke a few breaks to graze, he could almost feel the gelding's weariness. Rock Springs was a large railroad town and Clint was determined to buy grain there for his horse and have it curried and cared for even if that meant losing a few more hours.

His second surprise came just a few miles later as he neared town. A cry went up from the Rock Springs railroad station where a crowd was gathered and then, faintly in the distance, Clint heard his name being called. Moments later, there was a stampede of newspaper reporters running out to meet him.

"Well, I'll be damned," he said as much to himself as to the gelding. "We must have just got back into this horse race. There can't be any other reason for all this fuss."

He was right. When the mass of newspaper reporters reached him and Duke, they were all shouting questions so fast that it was almost impossible to understand any of them. Finally, Clint just yanked his gun out of his holster and fired three shots into the air to quiet the bunch.

"Now," he said. "If I understand you fellas, Iron Soldier took sick and Holloway is still in Rock Springs. Is that the way of it?"

They all agreed that it was, nodding their heads up and down, babbling so fast that Clint could not understand any of them.

"Hold it!" he yelled. "I'll answer a question after you ask one. But let's take it one at a time! Me first. Now, is Iron Soldier out of the running?"

"No," a reporter from Springfield, Illinois, shouted, "in fact, he's been resting for better than ten hours and he's about ready to go. Will you and Holloway ride out together? Make great headlines."

"Depends on how soon the man leaves," Clint said. "My horse needs a good feed and brushing. He's going to get both before we go on. But at least now we have a horse race, don't we?"

The reporters cheered for, indeed, now they had a real horse race. Clint rode Duke up to the Rock Springs livery.

"They won't let you inside," a reporter said. "Iron Soldier is in there but Holloway has some guards and they've denied us entry. As for your own horse, well, there appears to be another livery at the other end of town. But it looks like its ready to fall down."

"Then this is the one that will care for my horse," Clint said, riding up to the door and kicking it open with his stirrup.

He saw Iron Soldier and the veterinarian along with about a half dozen guards at the same moment that Iron Soldier twisted his neck around and spotted Duke. Iron Soldier stomped the ground and laid back his ears and tried to turn and rush the gelding but could not break free of the halter.

"Hey!" a guard yelled, "get that horse out of here!"

WINNER TAKE ALL 95

Clint dismounted. "I guess I won't ask this horse to go another foot. If you want Iron Soldier to have a barn all to himself, find another."

The guards advanced threateningly and they were a rough-looking bunch. With a knot still throbbing on the back of his head, Clint was in no mood to take another beating. So he just drew his six-gun and pointed it in their general direction. "I don't suppose any of you boys would admit knowing three men led by an ugly fella named Spike?"

When none of them answered, Clint said, "Well, Spike and his friends—your friends, too, I'll bet—they're pushing up prairie sod at Salt Wells. If any of you men would like to join them in hell, then be my guest and make your play. There's six of you and I've got six bullets, one for each. Don't worry, I won't miss."

The men hesitated in mid-stride. One raised his hands and then the others followed suit; it was clear that they were shocked to hear about Spike and the other two that Holloway had sent back to Salt Wells. With that grim piece of news fresh in their minds, they had no intention of testing the Gunsmith's mettle. "You can stay if you want," one of them rumbled. "It's a big damned barn anyway."

"I'm glad you're an intelligent bunch of men," Clint said, motioning with his gun toward the barn doors. The guards pushed outside and blocked the reporters from entering. Clint didn't mind. Both he and Duke needed a few quiet hours of rest. They'd never get it with a barn full of journalists.

"What about me?" the veterinarian asked. "It's my job to take care of this horse and he's been pretty sick up until the last couple of hours. Until Mr. Holloway rides him out, he bears close watching."

"Then stay with him," Clint said, dismounting and then

unsaddling the gelding. He ignored the veterinarian as he found a couple of burlap feed sacks and began to rub Duke's back.

"Is your gelding sore in the back?" the man asked.

"Wouldn't any horse be?" Clint asked. "We've come a long way in a short time."

"He looks better than I'd expected he would. You're the one that looks like hell."

Clint forced a wry grin. "Thanks. Where do they keep the oats in this place?"

"Over there. If I were you, I'd be sure not to give him more than a couple of quarts. Pour a couple more in your saddle bags and give it to him on the trail. Too much grain will make him as colicky as the Iron Soldier was last evening."

Clint put his horse into a stall and found the grain. He scooped up a couple of quarts and gave it to the black gelding, who devoured it like he was starving.

The veterinarian said, "There's some real good hay up in the loft. I'd give him all he wants to eat along with plenty of water."

Clint looked oddly at the veterinarian. "How come you're giving me helpful advice? I'm the enemy, remember?"

"The only thing I care about is these horses," the veterinarian said, moving over to the stall to observe Duke more closely. "You mind if I listen to his heart?"

Clint shrugged. "Take a listen."

The large man with the red face and little glasses entered the stall and, speaking quietly to Duke, he moved up to the horse, bent, and laid his ear against Duke's chest. He closed his eyes and listened. When he was satisfied, he ran his hands down all four of Duke's legs, from knee to the hoof.

"Well?"

"He's as sound as gold," the man said. "A remarkable animal. But then, until Mr. Holloway decided that the Iron Soldier could subsist on grain alone, so was the stallion."

"Is that why he's still here?"

"It is. But the gray has completely recovered, I'm almost sorry to admit."

Clint was puzzled. "Why?"

"Because this race is insane and before it is over, I fully expect at least one of these two magnificent animals to be crippled and destroyed."

"I won't let that happen to Duke," Clint vowed. "There is nothing that is worth ruining that gelding."

The veterinarian smiled tolerantly. "I wish I could believe you. But I'm just afraid that, when the race is on the line, you'll do anything to win. Anything."

"You're wrong," Clint said. "I've been insulted and challenged and I would like to win a pile of Holloway's money. But not bad enough to hurt Duke."

"Then you haven't a chance of winning, Mr. Adams. You see, these two horses are both exceptional animals. They've got the strength, speed and the heart to run forever. They'll explode their organs before they'll quit. So the winner of this race depends upon the man that also has enough heart and the determination to match his horse. Mr. Holloway qualifies on that score. I guess you don't and, therefore, are to be congratulated."

Clint frowned. "You're—"

He did not finish his statement, because the barn door swung open, and Vicki and Shorty came pushing their way past Holloway's guards. Right behind Vicki was a tall, somewhat handsome young man dressed in an expensive suit and wearing a bowler, a white shirt, and a starched collar.

Vicki flew into Clint's arms and hugged his neck. "It's so good to see you!" she cried. "I just *knew* you'd catch up with us!"

"Never mind him," Shorty growled, "how's the horse?"

"Ask the doc," Clint said, beckoning toward the veterinarian.

Holloway's private veterinarian said, "Duke is in remarkably good shape, but he's lost about a hundred pounds."

"I don't need no damned vet to tell me that!" Shorty groused, running his hands over the gelding's legs and then his back and withers. "Give him all the grain he'll eat!"

But the veterinarian shook his head. "He'd really be better off taking it in moderation."

"What?" Shorty cried. "Why, I—"

"That's enough!" Clint shouted, ending the argument. "Where's Holloway?"

"He's been sleeping over at the hotel," Vicki said, "but I'm sure that he'll be awakened by his men and come rushing over to see you."

Bobby Bouchard cleared his throat. "So," he said, "you are the famous Gunsmith. I've never met a cold-blooded killer before. A man who lives by the smoking revolver dealing death from his fist." Bouchard smiled without warmth. "You don't look so menacing."

"Who the hell is this jerk?" Clint asked.

Vicki made the introductions and as soon as they were over, Bouchard said, "I'd like an exclusive interview with you, Gunsmith."

"Adams," Clint said tersely. "Clint Adams."

"Very well, though you have to admit that 'the Gunsmith' does evoke a much livelier image. The fact of the matter is that Mr. Holloway has gotten all the press so far, while you have been quite obscure. Now that you have overtaken Iron Soldier, I think the world would be very interested in hearing more about you and your black horse."

"Sorry," Clint said, taking Vicki's arm and heading for the door. "Shorty, you stay here and watch over Duke, huh?"

"I'll do that!" the old man snorted. "You just watch yourself. There are a lot of Holloway's friends that arrived in town on that train."

Bouchard jumped on that. "Are you insinuating the possibility of foul play?"

Clint stopped at the door and whirled. "There's a lot more than 'insinuation' here. One of my horse's shoes was tampered with and I was braced by three men back at Salt Wells Station. I can't prove anything, but I can tell you this much, I'll bet anything they were sent by Max Holloway to stop me."

Max Holloway chose that exact moment to make his entrance. "My, my," he said, looking ruffled but rested after a ten-hour layover. He turned to the reporters and raised his hands palms up, the picture of the wronged man. "So now, I'm being accused of dealing in foul play. Surely none of you are going to stoop to such a low level as to print that groundless accusation, are you?"

"I might," Bouchard said. The publisher lifted his chin and it was plain to see that the pair did not like each other. Clint had a strong suspicion that Max saw Bouchard as yet another in a series of rivals for Vicki Flower's affections. "I will print it as a quote from Mr. Adams. Merely as an opinion, not a fact."

"It's a bald-faced lie is what it is," Max said, his voice taking on a hard edge.

Clint stiffened. "I think you had better retract that last statement."

"I'll be damned if I will!"

"And damned if you do not."

Vicki pushed between them. "Stop it!" she cried as the newspaper reporters scribbled furiously. "This is a horse race, not an invitation to a gunfight."

"Gunfight?" Max said, raising his eyebrows. "How ridiculous of you, my dear woman, to think that I'd be stupid enough to swap bullets with a professional killer."

Clint wanted to grab the man by the throat, but he restrained himself. Max turned to his veterinarian. "Is my horse ready?"

"Two more hours, Mr. Holloway."

"But he looks just fine!"

"What he looks like on the outside doesn't say what's going on with his insides," the veterinarian said stubbornly. "You can saddle and ride him out now, but he may colic right away. Give him just a few more hours and he'll have a better chance. It's a long race to go yet."

Max was not pleased and yet, as the newspaper reporters pushed around them and fired off questions, it must have occurred to him that the Gunsmith's arrival had created a great deal of excitement that had sorely been lacking when it had seemed as if the horse race was over almost before it had started.

"All right," he conceded. "I'll wait a few more hours. Vicki, would you care to join me for something to eat?"

"No, Max, I would not!" She hugged Clint's arm and then she linked her other arm through Bobby Bouchard's. "We've got things to discuss."

The Wyoming horse rancher stiffened. "You're making a real mistake," he said. "Adams has nothing and Bouchard has too much to waste it on someone of your low social standing. I'm the one that's right for you, Vicki. You've just forgotten how good we were together at night."

Vicki slapped his cheek. Hard. His lips cracked and he smiled, then found a silk handkerchief in his back pocket

WINNER TAKE ALL

and smeared the blood across his chin. "You always were a wildcat," he said, turning and walking out of the barn a moment before Clint decided to punch away that superior smile. "I liked it then, I like it now."

Clint, Vicki, and Bobby Bouchard left a few minutes later. Clint was not pleased to share a scant couple of hours of Vicki's company with the pompous newspaper publisher, and he guessed that Bouchard wasn't pleased with the arrangement either. But on the bright side, he was bushed and if they had been alone together, Vicki might have wanted to make love and he doubted that he'd have had the strength to deny her.

So maybe it was better this way after all. And if Bouchard rubbed his fur the wrong way too hard, Clint reckoned he could take care of that problem, too.

FOURTEEN

They had just finished eating dinner and then Bobby Bouchard had insisted on picking up the bill which, normally, would have pleased Clint just fine. The problem was that he did not like Bouchard. The man was conceited and a braggart. The publisher liked to let everyone know that he was rich and quite important. Yet, under all that bluster and noise, Clint suspected Bouchard was a man who could not stand on his own merits, but instead, like a parasite, had to such his worth out of others.

"So, Mr. Adams, that's my life story," he said, waving his wine glass and calling for more. "And I've heard Miss Flower's, so what's yours?"

Clint saw Vicki's half-smile. She could tell that Clint did not like this man, but she wasn't about to say so. "I'm a gunsmith. I was a lawman and now I fix guns and play a little cards. I like to travel."

Bouchard raised his eyebrows. "Don't be so modest. Modesty gets a man nothing in this world. You're a famous man. If you can somehow win this race, I can also make you rich."

Clint leaned back in his chair. "Rich, huh? What would I have to do for my money? Join one of them Wild West Shows and pretend to gun down the bad guys or maybe a couple of thousand reservation Indians?"

Bouchard's cheeks colored enough to tell Clint that he had pegged it right. "Hickok and Cody did very well for themselves. Very well indeed. And they did so because they understood the value of publicity. You ought to take a lesson from them, Mr. Adams. My paper could make you world-famous if you consented to an exclusive interview. Perhaps we could even stage a few mock gunfights. I don't know if Wyatt Earp or John Wesley Harding or any of those men would care to brace you, but if we—"

"Not interested," Clint said, cutting him off short.

Vicki touched his arm. "Clint, please don't be so hasty. There is nothing wrong with a little publicity and wealth. My ex-husband is a master at it and he's done very well."

"It's not my style," Clint said stubbornly. "There have been plenty of newspaper reporters and dime novelists who have wanted me to tell them all the bloody details of each gunfight I've won, each man I've shot. And when I say 'details', I mean they want to know how the man's face looked as he was dying, how his blood pumped from his chest, how hard he hit the dirt, and the sounds he made, whether or not there was a death rattle in his throat, or just a sigh as his lungs expelled their last breath."

Bouchard frowned. "I don't think that sort of thing is necessary. Really, I don't. What I was thinking was that we could stage a gunfight and then have your victim scream, grab his chest, smear catsup on his shirt, then reel around and fall."

"Yes, Clint," Vicki said. "That sounds very dramatic."

Clint shook his head. He was disappointed that Vicki didn't understand him any better than to approve of such a pathetic scheme. Tossing money for his own dinner on the table, he said, "I guess I'd better get back to Duke. He's probably had time to eat his fill Max Holloway ought to be getting ready to ride out any time now. I'd like to stick with him at least until we reach Nevada territory."

Bouchard was miffed by his flat refusal. "Can you keep up with Iron Soldier?"

"Yeah." Clint smiled. "I don't know if you placed any money on this race, but if you did, it had better be on Duke. We're going to win this race."

"A lot of good it will do you if you refuse to reap the harvest of your victory," Bouchard complained. "At least Mr. Holloway understands the opportunity that awaits the victor."

Clint looked at Vicki, "I guess you and me have just discovered some things we don't see eye to eye about when it comes to fame and money."

"I don't ever want to be poor again," she declared.

"That's not likely," Clint said. "Not when you hang around with the likes of men like him and Max Holloway. So long, Vicki. It was fun while it lasted."

She nodded, sad that it was ending this way and yet not at all willing to get involved with a man who cared so little about material success. Up until Max had become a well-to-do, she'd been poor most all of her life and she wanted no part of that again. And while Bobby Bouchard might be loud and a boor, at least he commanded attention and respect.

She turned her back on the Gunsmith and raised her wine glass. Touching it to Bobby's, she said, "To success and money."

He grinned and his eyes drank in her beauty.

When Clint arrived back at the livery, Duke was saddled and ready. There was a huge crowd of reporters and spectators and the special train was blasting its whistle, telling all its westbound passengers that the race was about to resume and that they had better get on board.

WINNER TAKE ALL

"How is he?" Clint asked, seeing Iron Soldier's head over a crowd as the animal was being prepared to ride.

"He's fit," Shorty said. "I had the blacksmith check his shoes and he seems ready to run."

Clint patted the sleek animal and then scratched Duke behind the ears. The gelding nudged him playfully. Across the barn, Iron Soldier trumpeted his challenge and Duke tossed his head. His long black mane waved in defiance.

"Let's get this show underway," Clint said, checking his cinch and finding it tight. He mounted at almost the very same moment that Max did. The talk died and both men reined their horses toward the barn doors. Once outside, they rode side by side with photographers lining the streets and taking pictures as they passed. It seemed as if everyone in Rock Springs had turned out to see them race away.

"Let's give them a show," Clint said.

"I couldn't agree more," Max replied bringing his quirt down hard across the stallion's haunches.

Iron Soldier shot forward, ears back, front legs reaching out to gobble up the land stretching before them. The stallion had gotten the lead but in less than a mile, Clint had overtaken him and they both had drawn their two horses in and settled down to a long, swinging lope. Each man heard the train whistle blasting, and they knew that the iron monster was about to take up their trail.

Max looked over at him and yelled, "I noticed that my Vicki didn't give you any send-off. What happened?"

"None of your business."

Max laughed. "You don't have to tell me. Vicki loves a winner. If you win, and if you play the game, she's yours. But if I win, she'll come back to me."

"No she won't," Clint said with grim satisfaction. "Not if she can bag a rich millionaire for a husband."

Max's grin slipped badly. He turned away and looked

straight ahead with anger fomenting inside him. Bouchard was a babe in the western woods. The man might be rich, but out West, he was easy game to bag. And if he had any sense at all, he'd stay in Rock Springs and wait for the next train.

If Bobby Bouchard got serious about Vicki, the man was digging his own grave.

FIFTEEN

They had alternately galloped, trotted, and walked side by side all day crossing the famed Bridger Basin and then had faced the steep eastern slopes of the Wasatch Mountains. Surprisingly, the Gunsmith had come to enjoy Max Holloway's company. The man was ruthless and could not be trusted, but there was little doubt that he was brave, resourceful, and an excellent horseman. He could be amusing and did have some pretty funny stories to tell. He would have been good riding company if the situation had been different.

"These mountains will take its toll on your gelding," he said as they galloped up into the foothills. "You've got too heavy a saddle and your horse isn't conditioned the way that mine is. Besides, when it comes to stamina, there has never been a gelding that could stand up to a stud. When they lose their balls, they lose a measure of grit."

"We'll just see about that," Clint said, leaning forward in the stirrups so that he could position his weight over Duke's withers and give the animal every bit of advantage he could.

Duke responded with all the heart that Clint had come to expect from the horse after years of their being together. The black gelding, though carrying more weight, simply refused to be left in Iron Soldier's dust. So as they started up the steeper slopes, both men and horses were a study of concentration, each attempting to be a perfectly synchronized operating unit.

They climbed three thousand feet and both horses were puffing hard when Clint pulled Duke up for a breather. Max went on a few yards, then he also reined the gray in and dismounted. He looked down at Clint. "You're staying up with us far better than I would have imagined. For a gelding, he's a hell of a horse."

"I know," Clint said, loosening Duke's cinch so that the animal could breath easier. "Iron Soldier isn't bad, either."

Max stood with one boot on the railroad tracks and the other on a railroad tie. He shaded his eyes and reached into the mochila to retrieve a spy glass. He telescoped it out and, closing one eye, he peered back at the country they had just ridden across.

"You looking for something in particular," Clint asked, "or are you just looking?"

"I'm looking for smoke in the air that will tell me how far the train is behind us," Max said. "And I found it. About six miles down that canyon that dog-legs to the right. They'll be going up this mountainside even slower than us. But they'll come down a whole lot faster."

"Once we get over these mountains, the Great Salt Lake Basin is going to be hot," Clint said. "I guess you know that the Paiutes are raisin' hell out there."

"Yeah, I know. That's why I plan to stay out in front and keep the train close to me. By then, I'll have left you far behind."

"We'll just have to see about that," Clint said. "If you haven't figured it out yet, this horse and I don't take seconds to anyone."

In answer, Max remounted and rode on, guiding his horse along the tracks. Clint waited another five minutes until his horse was breathing normal, then he retightened his cinch and climbed back into the saddle. He was dead tired but determined not to give the lead back to the Cheyenne horse rancher.

Over the Wasatch train tunnels built just under the summit, a band of outlaws waited. "Here they come," the outlaw leader named Frankie Pearl said as he and his men hunkered down. "The one in front is Holloway. I read he had the gray stallion. It's the guy about a half a mile behind him that's the Gunsmith. He's the fella we don't want to mess with."

Dick Wheat licked his chapped lips and nodded. He laid the barrel of his Winchester down on a rock and drew a bead on the second rider. "He shot a friend of mine once. I'd like to even the score."

But Frankie Pearl batted his rifle off target. "Don't be a fool! Even if you did make the shot and killed the Gunsmith, you'd have alerted the whole train!"

"So what?"

Pearl yanked the rifle from Wheat's hands. "So it's not the way we agreed to do this," he said. "We agreed that we'd let the riders pass and *then* we'd hit the train. There are supposed to be a lot of rich easterners on this one so it'll be like stealing candy from a baby. We block the tunnel at the west end, then close off the east and have 'em come out with their hands up in the air holding nothing but money. This is the one we've always been hoping for. I won't let you go and spoil it. You clear on that?"

Wheat nodded grudgingly. He feared Frankie Pearl and knew the man would gun him down in a stand-up fight. Frankie was a tall, buck-toothed, red-haired, chinless sonofabitch who had the fastest hands and most inhuman eyes Wheat had ever seen. Frankie Pearl was said to be part

Indian, part Irish but mostly rattlesnake and tarantula. He was a killer and he was ugly and smart.

"What about after we take the train?" Wheat asked.

"How are you going to catch up with the Gunsmith? The idea of this whole thing is to hit the train and clear out. Neither he or Holloway will even suspect what happened until they reach Ogden."

Wheat nodded. "I just hate to let him pass right through my rifle sights is all. I could drill him right through the buttons."

"You just drill that charge of dynamite we set above the western portal of the tunnel and block it off tight. After this job is over, you can take up the Gunsmith's trail and kill him when you want."

Pearl looked at the rest of his gang. They numbered ten and he knew that every man among them was tough and a crack shot. He had planned this train robbery from the very day he'd heard about the horse race and how it had warranted the Union Pacific making up a special train. Pearl had robbed trains before and each time he'd found that bullion was kept in a vault in the mail car and that the vault was too heavy to carry away and too well-made to break open. But this time, the money would be in the passenger's pockets. Oh, they'd go to the mail car and see if there was a vault or a strong box being transported, but mostly, Pearl figured that the big haul would be from the passengers themselves. Besides the millionaire Bouchard, there were several other wealthy men.

"Look at that!" Wheat hissed. "The gray won't go into the tunnel."

Pearl nodded. "If he has to come around, he might try and come on over the top and we'll have to kill him."

"Be a damned shame. And I guess that we'd have to kill

WINNER TAKE ALL   111

the Gunsmith as well, 'cause he'd hear the shots and probably come to investigate.''

Pearl frowned. ''You just better hope that doesn't happen. I've heard plenty enough stories about that man's fighting that I don't want to tangle with him unless there is no other choice. But look at him just trotting that big black along as if he hadn't a care in the world. He sure doesn't act like a man in a horse race, does he?''

''No,'' Wheat said, ''he sure does not.''

Clint saw Max and the gray up ahead and the dark tunnel they faced. He'd known that they'd have to go through a tunnel and that there might be a problem. A horse just naturally didn't like to enter a dark hole in the mountainside. Probably it was an instinctual thing, where they realized that bears and mountain cats used caves as lairs. Whatever the reason, Iron Soldier was refusing his rider and giving Clint plenty of time to catch up.

''Seems like you've got a big problem,'' Clint said, riding up to the pair. ''Maybe you ought to dismount and lead him on through.''

Max dismounted in a huff. He slung the reins over the stallion's head and tried to lead him into the tunnel but the horse still refused. ''Goddam you!''

Clint rode Duke up the railroad tunnel. It was so long and crooked that he could barely see a glimmer of sunlight poking through the far end. He nudged Duke with his heels. ''Come on now,'' he said. ''It isn't that bad.''

Duke pricked his ears forward and snorted with apprehension but he stepped forward and his hoofs made a hollow sound as they entered the tunnel.

''Hey!'' Max shouted. ''You just going to leave me here? That isn't fair!''

Clint chuckled and rubbed Duke's neck. It amused him that Max Holloway could talk about fairness. After all, the man had sent three hired gunnies to Salt Wells to have him stopped.

Duke felt like he was walking on eggs as he pranced forward toward the strengthening light. Clint could hear Max shouting and cussing back at the entrance to the tunnel and then, a few minutes later, Max's voice was gone. Duke passed on through the tunnel and when he came out on the western portal, Clint turned in his saddle and peered back into the tunnel. Seeing or hearing nothing, he guessed that Max Holloway had been forced to go around the tunnel, which would not be easy. He'd either have to dodge the edge around a very dangerous drop-off below the tracks, or he'd have to climb around the tunnel. Clint did not care which choice Max Holloway opted for. All that mattered was that, for the first time since this race began, he was in the lead.

"Come on," he said to Duke as he touched his heels to the animal's flanks. "Let's put some ground between us and him."

Duke broke into an easy canter and Clint would not have even bothered to look back except that he heard a gunshot, then several more which followed in rapid succession.

He pulled his horse up and wheeled around just in time to see Max Holloway flying off the summit ridge as if he were being chased by a swarm of yellow jackets. Only instead of yellow jackets, Clint saw the band of outlaws. He drew his gun and went to meet Max. "What happened?"

"I don't know!" Max shouted. "I had no choice but to ride over the summit and I practically rode over the top of them. One minute I was alone, the next all hell was breaking out."

"Give me your eyeglass," Clint ordred.

When he had it, Clint scanned the summit. "I don't see them anymore," he said, handing the glass back to Max.

"Well, they're not our problem. Let's just git!"

But Clint shook his head. "They must be planning to rob the train. There's no reason why that many men would be up on the summit, but—"

Suddenly, a man popped up from behind a rock with a rifle in his hands and took a long, steady aim on something down near the western portal where Clint had just emerged from the tunnel. The rifle cracked and almost in the same instant, there was a huge explosion over the tunnel exit.

"Holy cow!" Max shouted, as rocks and dirt pelted them. "What are they up to now!"

"It's simple enough to figure," Clint said. "They're going to rob the train."

"But it isn't carrying any payroll!"

"No," Clint said, "it isn't. But it is carrying some pretty well-heeled journalists, not the least of whom is Bobby Bouchard."

Max threw back his head and laughed. "Bouchard being robbed . . . now *that* I'd like to see! Let them guys have him! All it will do is make us even better publicity. In fact, I couldn't have planned for anything more dramatic."

Clint was not nearly so delighted. "What if they kill someone or take a hostage? Maybe even Vicki? Will that strike you as amusing or hilarious?"

Max stopped grinning but his decision to go on had not changed. "If they take her, they'll get more than they bargained for. Vicki is a hell of a woman, enough of one to handle any man. I say let her stand or fall on her own. Neither of us owes her anything. When it came right down to it in Rock Springs, she chose the man with the most money. I'm riding on."

"And I'm turning back," Clint said. "I'm not going to

walk away from train robbery that is about to take place."

Max was furious. "Goddammit! You're not being paid to play hero. If you go back and I ride on, then I'll look like a heel or even a coward. But if we both ride on we can just claim we didn't know anything about the robbery. The train will catch up with us and those reporters will go crazy trying to file their stories out of Ogden."

"It doesn't work that way with me," Clint said, reining Duke about and starting back.

"Damn you!" Max shouted. "I hope they kill you!"

Clint said nothing. He could see smoke and dust pouring out of the tunnel's mouth and as it cleared and it was apparent that the outlaws had not done a very good job at setting their dynamite charge. There were some huge boulders that had fallen across the tracks, but if the idea had been to drop the tunnel ceiling and thus prevent the train from coming through, then the outlaws had done a mighty poor job.

A bullet wanged off the steel rails just ahead of Clint and it made a sharp, mean sound. Clint pulled his own Winchester from his boot scabbard and levered a shell in the breech. He glanced back and saw that Max was galloping on ahead. To hell with him! Clint thought. I can do this better alone.

SIXTEEN

Before he came into the outlaw's accurate rifle range, Clint dismounted and tied Duke in some thickets near the tracks. Then, weaving and dodging, he ran forward with bullets whining off the tracks and rocks all around him. When he reached the western portal, he found safety, for the outlaws above could no longer see him. Because of the dynamite blast and attempt to block the tunnel, dust made it hard to breathe and impossible to see. Tying a bandanna over his face, he hurried forward, intent on reaching the eastern portal and flagging down the train. Once inside the summit tunnel, the locomotive engineer would not be able to see the fallen boulders until it was too late to stop. The train would crash into the rocks and it might even derail.

Clint had almost run the length of the tunnel when he saw the outlaws suddenly emerge in the round orb of sunlight just up ahead. The Gunsmith threw his rifle to his shoulder and pulled the trigger. His rifle shot sounded like cannon fire in the close confines of rock walls and a man went down to stay. Before Clint could unleash another round, the others jumped sideways for cover. A moment later, they stuck their six-guns around the rocks and fired blindly into the tunnel.

Clint hugged the rock walls as bullets ricocheted back

and forth the length of the tunnel. He knew he would be crazy to charge forward because there were too many of them to take on all by himself. And yet, he could not afford to remain where he was and let the train come thundering into the tunnel.

The Gunsmith knelt down and took a steady aim with his rifle. When a gun clenched in someone's hand edged into view, Clint shot the hand. He heard a scream and the gun went flying.

Clint grinned to himself. Now, he thought, they won't be so ready to try that trick.

He heard the Union Pacific's steam whistle blast and started forward again. He was confident that the outlaws would want to stay hidden until the train passed them and plunged into the tunnel. Clint ran straight for the entrance of the tunnel determined to beat the train and give it some warning. When he reached the opening, he tossed aside his six-gun and jumped out into the sunlight. The outlaws were caught by surprise and he managed to kill three before the rest scattered into the rocks just as the train rounded a bend and blasted into view.

"No!" Clint yelled, waving his arms. "Stop!"

He heard the train's brakes lock instantly followed by the terrible shriek of steel grinding steel. But Clint had given his warning too late. The train was traveling much too fast and was far too heavy to stop in time and Clint had to jump sideways to avoid being run down as the locomotive shot into the tunnel, locked wheels sending off showers of sparks so bright that it seemed as if the tunnel had been transformed by the light of the sun.

Moments later, Clint heard a tremendous crash as the locomotive struck the massive boulders blocking its path. The train seemed to shiver like a shot rattlesnake and then

WINNER TAKE ALL

it ground to a tortuous halt. Almost at once, Clint heard shouts of fear and terror from the passengers. He ignored them, huddled down, retrieved his six-gun, ready to kill the first outlaw foolish enough to show his face.

Two jumped out onto the track, both with guns. One of them started to shout something, but he died with the message in his throat. Before the second outlaw coiuld leap aside, Clint shot him, too.

The train passengers who had already disembarked from the train hit the rock floor at the sound of gunfire. When it died, they climbed back into their coaches. If they'd assumed that the train had simply struck an errant boulder, they now knew better.

Clint moved swiftly to the mouth of the tunnel, but when he edged outside, a spray of bullets sent him tumbling back for cover.

"What's going on?" Shorty and several others who came running up behind him yelled.

"We're trapped," Clint said. "There's still seven or eight of them out there waiting for us to stick our necks out and make an easy target."

"Well we sure as hell can't stay in here!"

Clint holstered his six-gun. "Hello out there! What do you want!"

"Money!" came the answer. "Everyone on the train throw down your weapons and come out with your hands up holding your money and jewelry."

Shorty yanked his six-gun out of his holster. "I'll give 'em my answer!" he snarled.

But Clint grabbed him. "No," he said. "We can't beat them by rushing into their guns. We have to outsmart them."

"How?" Clint recognized Vicki's voice.

"You do as they say while I go back out the other end

and sneak up and over the summit to get the drop on them."

"You can't do it alone! Let me go with you. I'm a good shot."

"No," Clint said. "Too dangerous. And Shorty, don't you even volunteer. You're too crippled to make it over the top without me carrying you. And I don't think I have the strength for it."

"Where is Max Holloway?" Bobby Bouchard demanded.

"He went on."

"Figures," the publisher said. "I happen to have been a marksman on my college team. I suppose honor permits me no alternative but to go with you."

"Shooting at targets and shooting at men who shoot back are entirely different," Clint said. "Forget about honor. I need someone I can rely upon in a tight fix."

"I'll do my best not to cut and run from the face of enemy fire," the publisher said. "And if we survive, this will make cracking good copy."

"Anyone else?" Clint asked, addressing the collection of passengers.

He had no other volunteers. "All right then, the rest of you play it as they say. Go out one at a time with your hands up and don't anyone try any foolishness. We should be over the summit in about ten minutes and we'll catch them from behind and by surprise. When the shooting starts, everyone hit the dirt and stay down."

"Not me," Shorty said. "I got a sawed-off shotgun in the coach I'm going to get and I'll step out firin' both damn barrels. Where's our horse?"

"He's safe," Clint assured the old man.

"Vicki, you stay back."

"No, I'm still coming with you. Max taught me how to shoot straight and I can climb rocks as good as either of you."

"Why not let her come if she wishes?" Bouchard said. "I think we can use all the help we can get."

Clint didn't like the idea but he could not argue with the man's reasoning. "All right," he said. "Come along then. The rest of you, start filing out, but slowly, and one at a time."

Clint whirled and ran back into the tunnel, following the train and finally staggering past the locomotive. When he came to the west end of the tunnel, he skidded to a halt and reloaded his six-gun. "Let's go," he said, edging outside and starting to climb through the scree of fallen rocks created by the dynamite explosion.

It was hard, treacherous work because the rocks were like loose shale and sometimes they would slip two feet for every yard they managed. But finally, chests heaving, leg muscles burning, they did reach the summit, and they slipped into the rocks and peered down at the scene far below.

The outlaws had the passengers out and lined up. There seemed to be a hundred people with their hands in the air, but they were still filing out and Clint did not see Shorty yet.

"No point in hesitating now," he said, starting down the mountainside.

Bouchard was not so sure. "Now wait a minute," he whispered, "let's talk this over. Perhaps the outlaws will give up when they see that we have the drop on them."

"Would you give up if you numbered seven and the people telling you to drop your guns only numbered three?"

"Well . . . well, yes!"

"They won't," Clint said, moving forward again. "Just don't fire until I do."

Vicki nodded. She looked pale and scared but Clint felt sure that her nerve would not break and that she would back him up if things got rough. Bobby Bouchard was another matter altogether. Maybe he had been a collegiate marksman, but that didn't hold much importance out here. But at least the man had had the presence of mind to bring a gun.

They were moving down through the trees and rocks, trying to get as close as possible to the rear of the outlaws, when Bobby Bouchard tripped over a branch and pitched into a rolling dive that carried him and a small landslide of rocks headlong down the mountainside.

The outlaws looked up in surprise and not only saw Bobby, but also Clint and Vicki. "Take cover!" Clint shouted as he opened fire.

Vicki threw herself beind some rocks and the passengers below scattered like quail. Most jumped back into the tunnel but some, in their sheer panic, leapt right over off the lip of the mountainside.

Shorty played his role to perfection. He stepped out of the tunnel and unleashed two murderous volleys from his shotgun that took three outlaws out at once. Clint and Vicki downed the others.

The battle did not last more than a few seconds. The gunfire echoed up and down the narrow canyon until everything was suddenly very still.

"We did it," Vicki said. "We did it!"

Clint smiled. "Yeah. And the tunnel should be easy enough to clear away once everyone puts their minds to the task. Maybe you had better go down and see if Bouchard broke his neck or not."

She nodded. "He took an awful fall. But at least he tried."

"Yeah," Clint said. "At least he tried."

She touched his cheek as he started to turn away. "Clint, I know you don't understand me. But I don't understand you, either! You've got this chance to become really rich and famous if you'd just listen to Bobby. But you act as if he was trying to change you in some way."

"He would be," Clint said. "He'd make a mockery of

what I stood for all those years I was a lawman. He'd have me dressed in white like Wild Bill and I'd feel like a buffoon. No thanks, Vicki. Money isn't that important to me. It never has been."

"But it is to me!"

"Then marry him if you can. You were once married to Max Holloway and he got rich. I'd think that should have taught you a lesson or two."

She lowered her eyes. "Yes, I guess it should have. But I've never been one to learn my lessons well. So go on and find your horse, Clint Adams. Race after Max and beat the pants off of him!"

Clint smiled. "We'll do our best. Vicki?"

She turned.

"Thanks," he said quietly. "And tell old Shorty the same for me."

She nodded and then, as the journalists stared at them and came to their feet, Vicki started down the mountainside.

SEVENTEEN

When Max Holloway reached Odgen, he felt almost certain that Clint Adams would be dead and the train derailed. Max was shaken and not at all sure if he was happy with the way things had turned out. He had wanted to win the race at any cost, but what good would it do if he won by default? And without the special train to chronicle his historic ride and victory, there seemed little point in going on. And yet . . . yet there was always the chance that Adams and the train had overcome the outlaws and would come charging down the western slope of the Wasatch bigger than life. And finally, there was Vicki to think about. What if the outlaws had done something to her? It wasn't likely, but she was a very beautiful woman, probably the only beautiful woman on that train and men were men. Max knew that he had to do something besides just going on.

"I want to send a telegraph message," he said, rushing into the Western Union office. "Wire San Francisco and Omaha that the Union Pacific train has been attacked at the Wasatch tunnels and probably derailed."

The telegraph operator looked up at him, eyes round with surprise. "Are you sure?"

"Of course I am! Send the damned message."

"Well, I can send it east, but not west to San Francisco."

WINNER TAKE ALL

"Why not?"

"Paiutes are on the warpath again. They cut the telegraph lines down. The eastbound express is eight hours overdue and we're thinking they might even have derailed it somewhere between here and Reno."

Max swore long and loud. When he finished, he said, "Well, send the damned telegraph to Union Pacific headquarters in Omaha! And you can say that Max Holloway is pushing on to complete this thousand-mile race."

The telegraph operator blinked. "You're Mr. Holloway?"

"I am."

"Well, where's the Gunsmith?"

"Hell if I know. Back somewhere in those mountains. This is a horse race, man! I'm winning it and I sure don't have time to keep track of the loser. Now send the message as I've ordered and be quick about it."

The telegraph operator was young and chubby and when he nodded his jowls quivered. He wore a green eyeshade and his hair was thin. "Mr. Holloway, I gotta tell you that you better end that race right here and now. Nobody in their right mind would ride west without having a whole damned regiment of cavalry surrounding them."

"Hold that message a minute," Max said. "I need to think this out."

"Wise decision, Mr. Holloway. I know you're brave, but—"

"Oh, shut up and let me think!"

"Yes sir."

Max turned away and began to pace up and down the floor. If he took this man's advice—and he was sure it was sound—then he could walk away from this race neither a winner or a loser. No one would fault him for not going on in the face of a Paiute uprising. But it wasn't his nature to quit a thing, especially when the clear truth of the matter was that the greater the danger and risks, the greater the glory if he did make it to Carson City.

"I remember when the Pony Express was shut down east of here," he said, as much to himself as to the telegraph operator who waited anxiously for his decision. "I was mad and so was Kit Carson and Pony Bob Haslam. We always figured that we could outrun any damned Indians who came after us. But we had our orders so we shut down for a week. I was always sorry about that."

He made up his mind. "I got a faster horse now than I ever had then. I can still outrun any Indians I might come across! Send that telegram to Omaha and tell the world that Maxwell Holloway is going on alone into the face of danger and he will prevail!"

"But . . . but, sir!"

Max walked over to the operator and grabbed his shirtfront and shook him hard. "I gave you an order. Now do it!"

The man's jowls quivered and he gulped noisily. "Yes sir!"

Max spun on his heel and went out the door. He stopped at the livery just long enough to grain and water Iron Soldier, then he bought a carbine at the general store and prepared to ride out alone. By that time, a crowd had gathered and other men were trying to convince him that it was crazy to go on with the race.

"Mr. Holloway, wait!"

Max had been just about to mount his stallion and ride out when a man came rushing up with a pencil and paper in hand. "My name is Otis Washington of the *Ogden Daily Chronicle*. Is it true you intend to push on alone?"

"It is."

"But surely you've been told of the Indian depredations to the east of us."

WINNER TAKE ALL

"I have. But I'm going anyway. I figure Americans need western heroes. And maybe I don't quite measure up to Davy Crockett and those who died at the Alamo, but when I start something, I mean to finish it. That's the spirit of the men who built this great country."

Max watched the man scribbling down his words, for he wanted to make sure the editor got them right. Satisfied, he continued. "I rode the Pony Express when I was a young man and I have to say that I stood equal to the greatest of the riders of the Plains. Now, I'm here to prove that Iron Soldier is the finest horse that ever bred a mare in this country or raced a thousand miles across hostile country."

"Courageous words, Mr. Holloway. May I quote you?"

"You'd damn sure better," he said, climbing onto his gray stallion. Max took off his white Stetson and waved it overhead in a circle. "If by chance the man known as 'the Gunsmith' should arrive, I hope you good people will try to convince him that he should give up this race. There's no reason two brave men should risk their lives."

"Well spoken!" the editor shouted as the people of Ogden cheered in agreement.

Max touched spurs to Iron Soldier and raced away. He was smiling. He could see the many worshipful faces looking up at him and he was proud that he had made the right decision. Now, all he had to do was to survive and manage to get across about six hundred miles of desolation and danger.

He leaned forward and patted his horse's neck. "We can do it, big fella. You can outrun any Indian pony that ever lived."

The stallion's ears flickered back and forth as if in answer, and Odgen faded in the distance behind them.

EIGHTEEN

Darkness fell swiftly as Max followed the railroad tracks west out of Ogden toward historic Promontory Point where the Union Pacific and the Central Pacific had joined to link the nation and create the first transcontinental railroad. It had been the goddam telegraph, quickly followed by the transcontinental railroad that had put the Pony Express out of business, Max reminded himself.

The night sky slowly filled with stars and the desert's temperature plummeted. Max reined Iron Soldier down to an easy jog and his mind drifted back to those great days when he'd ridden this country. He remembered how exhilarated he'd felt racing into a station, flying off his lathered pony with the mochila in hand and vaulting onto the back of another horse held in wait. Just a shout from the hostler and that was all before he was leaving the man in the dust and settling into a new run. Damn! Back then, he felt as if he could have ridden around the world if there had been no oceans and a lot more fast horses.

But now, he felt sore, weary and worried. He was not young anymore, though not old. Still, he ached and the insides of his legs were starting to chafe. Iron Soldier moved with his head down, purposefully but without any enthusiasm. It was clear that the horse was bone-tired. Maybe

... if the train ever did catch up with him, he could switch with that ringer gray and save the stallion. What good was a victory if he ruined the horse for future breeding? After all, wasn't that the purpose of this entire affair? That and gaining fame and winning Vicki back?

To hell with Vicki, he thought bitterly. She's trying to snag that millionaire from back East. Max clenched his teeth in anger at the mere thought of Vicki doing a thing like that. Well, maybe he could arrange a little accident to happen when they all reached Carson City. A fatal accident.

Somewhere out in the desert he heard a pack of coyotes howl. It was a lonesome sound and Max wished he were back in Cheyenne at the Stockman's House where he had friends to share a drink and swap lies with. "I'm feeling kind of sorry I talked us into this," he said to the stallion. "I guess . . ."

The horse stopped dead still in its tracks and the lament died in Max's throat. Iron Soldier's head was up now. His nostrils dilated and he snorted in fear. Max felt the hairs on the back of his head raise when the stallion suddenly wheeled around to face their backtrail.

Indians!

Max saw them following his tracks in the moonlight and his blood went cold, for there were at least twenty. Just dim, dim silhouettes against a curtain of gray. Perhaps a mile behind. Had they actually seen him yet? There was the possibility that they were simply following the tracks as he was going and were quite unaware that a white man was just up ahead.

Max swallowed noisily. His every instinct told him to run but reason prevailed, and he reined the stallion back to the west and touched spurs. The gray responded and fell into a ground eating lope that it could maintain for hours. Max kept looking around behind him until he could no longer see the silhouettes. He prayed that the Indians would veer off from the tracks before morning and never even see his stallion's hoofmarks on the hard gravel railroad bed.

Dawn found him miles beyond Promontory and out of water. The sun came up hot and once it was over the lip of the world, it seared the coolness from the land and all living things scuttled or darted for shade. But not him and Iron Soldier. No, they alone seemed to be the only creatures that were moving as the sun rose higher and higher.

Max kept twisting around in his saddle, always pulling out his spy glass and hunting for a faint plume of dust rising in the sky. Or maybe even of smoke signaling that the special train—his protection—was coming to his aid. But as the morning wore on, he saw neither dust nor smoke and soon, his thoughts turned more to water than to Indians.

This was a wretched land. To the south of him, shimmering like a mirror, lay the Great Salt Lake. So much water and yet so worthless to a thirsty man and his laboring horse. Max stared at the huge body of water and the vast salt and alkali flats that surrounded it for miles and miles. He watched heat waves undulate off the scorched desert floor and yearned for the green, green grass of Wyoming.

Iron Soldier stopped sweating about noon and Max knew that the stallion was in trouble. He dismounted and poured the last of the water in his canteen into his Stetson and cupped it under the gray's muzzle. The stallion inhaled the precious water and sucked for more. Max twisted up his expensive hat like a dishrag and wrang a few drops of water out for himself. He replaced the hat on his head, feeling hot and miserable.

"No shade out here," he muttered, staring at the northern shore of the Great Salt Lake and trying to imagine what

WINNER TAKE ALL

good such a stinking, stagnant body of water did anyone.

Max led his horse over to a low rise and then he tied it to some brush and walked the rest of the way up to scout his backtrail. They were still coming. Just as they had been coming after him since daybreak. There was simply no sense in kidding himself any longer. The Paiutes had spotted his trail and knew that they had a lone white man.

To the north, he could see the railroad tracks glinting in the sunlight and he decided that he might as well start angling northwest and try to reach them before the Indians overtook him. Not that he expected that the tracks would bring him any help, but a man clung to any small thread he could when things were desperate.

How many Indians were coming? The sand and the sage were so white and the sun so blinding that he could not be sure. On and off during the long morning, he had counted between six and eight. No more than ten, no less than five. What difference did an Indian or two make anyway? When they overtook him—and the way Iron Soldier was tying up from lack of water, that would be in a matter of hours—Max knew that he was going to be shot. Shot because he'd been foolish enough to leave a rifle behind, thinking that its weight would be too much of a critical factor.

The Gunsmith had elected to bring a rifle.

Max studied his horse. Its eyes seemed sunken a little and he wished it hadn't stopped sweating because that was always the sign that a horse had dehydrated and overheated so badly it would soon go into convulsions if it did not get water. "I've really messed things up," he said to the animal. "I should have gone back with the Gunsmith and taken my chances saving the train from them outlaws."

He remounted and reined northeast. When he looked back an hour later, sweat was stinging his eyes and the Indians were much closer. Max turned to gauge the distance to the tracks up ahead. What? Five miles? Seven? He could not be sure. All he knew was that it seemed important that he reach the tracks. There, he would make his stand. And if the Indians scalped and multilated him as they sometimes did so that the spirits of their enemies would not leave this world whole, then at least the Gunsmith and the people on the train would find his body and maybe they'd also find the bodies of a few Indians and know he'd died fighting.

Max urged his horse on. The animal felt loose in the legs and it weaved. He touched its muscular neck, then pinched the flesh and saw that it held a puckered ridge instead of tightened flat as it normally would. Iron Soldier was ready to go into convulsions. He doubted that he would even make it back to the railroad line.

But Iron Soldier surprised him. The gray stallion did reach the railroad bed and Max dismounted under a small trestle laid to span a gulley. It was a lousy place to make his stand but it was better than nothing.

The Indians were within a mile of him and they seemed to be in no hurry now that he had stopped and was preparing to fight. There was definitely seven of them and if that wasn't bad enough, they all carried rifles. Maybe only old single-shot percussion weapons, but rifles all the same.

Max sleeved sweat from his eyes and crouched down in the gully. He removed his cartridge belt and holster and laid it carefully alongside of him. The belt held another eight bullets so he had two for each of the Indians. Maybe he could do it. Somehow get ahold of a pony and race away. He'd have to leave the Iron Soldier, but the horse was finished anyway without water very soon.

A quarter mile away, the Indians stopped and went into a conference. Max watched them gesturing toward him and after about ten minutes, they seemed to reach a decision and it was one that did not greatly surprise him. The Indians split up and began to encircle him and the gully.

Max looked up at the sky. There was about an hour left of daylight. Unless he was mistaken, they'd wait until there was a blood-red sunrise to blind him and then they'd come swooping in at him from every angle. He'd get a few, though, before he went down, he'd make them earn his scalp.

NINETEEN

When Clint had ridden into Odgen, leading the train, it had been past midnight. Even so, Otis Washington of the *Odgen Daily Chronicle* had come rushing up with his pencil and notebook paper in hand. "Is it true that you were attacked by outlaws at the summit tunnel?" the newspaper man cried.

"We were," Clint had said, not stopping Duke but riding directly to a water trough where Duke promptly sank his muzzle and drank a prodigious amount of water.

"What a story!" Washington cried. "I want to know every detail."

But Clint had shaken his head. "The only way you could have known about the outlaws up there is by Max Holloway telling you. Where is he?"

"On his way to Reno. I tried to warn him of the Indian depredations we've had lately. Why, there are reports of Indians on the warpath all the way over to Elko. I told him he was crazy to go on alone without protection, but he's an extraordinarily brave man. He begged me to see if I could get you to stay in Ogden until this trouble is over."

"I'll just bet he did."

Clint had let Duke finish drinking his fill and then he had bought a five-gallon skin water bag. He'd looped the bag over the saddle and ridden out saying, "Mr. Washington, if you want a good story to write, ask the passengers and the train people about those outlaws. They can tell you as much of a story as I can."

It had been a long night and when daylight seeped timidly across the still, brush-covered land, Clint had realized that Max Holloway's tracks had been joined by those of Indian ponies. The tracks had led south and Clint had followed them all morning and afternoon. Now, it was late afternoon and the tracks were leading him back to the railroad line and they were less than an hour old.

Clint dismounted and poured water from the skin bag into his hat. When he and Duke had drunk enough, he closed the bag and looked east, wondering if the train had pulled out of Ogden and if it would be along soon. He imagined that Shorty, Vicki, and all the others were pretty upset the way he had just slipped out of town without even offering an explanation. But hell, he was tired of being asked so many questions and having his every move watched.

Clint tied off the skin bag and looped it back over his saddlehorn. He wondered how Max was carrying water since he had no horn or real saddle to tie water to; the fool had probably left Ogden with little more than a canteen.

He mounted and rode on, the setting sun now low on the western horizon and painfully bright in his eyes. He pulled his Stetson right down over his brow and that helped, but still, as the sunset deepened, the sage seemed to glisten like polished wire and he would be glad when it was down below the horizon.

Gunfire erupted somewhere ahead, and Clint yanked his rifle from under his knee. He knew from reading the tracks that seven Indians were following Max. Seven warriors made long odds, but then, he could not discount the fact that Max

Holloway might at least kill one or two and thus narrow the margin more to Clint's liking.

The sun was treacherous, but Clint let Duke have his head and the gelding ran nimbly over the sage and rocks without falling. When he flew over a low ridge, Clint squinted his eyes and saw the fight just ahead. He levered a shell into the breech of his rifle and leaned forward in his stirrups. Duke shot past a mounted warrior so suddenly that both Clint and the brave were caught by surprise. Half blinded by the setting sun, they each fired and missed. The difference was, however, that Clint's rifle was a repeater while the Indian's was not. The difference proved fatal for the Indian as Clint's second bullet knocked him spinning from his horse.

A moment later, Clint almost went airborne as Duke sailed off an embankment and seemed to hang in the air only to crash into a gully.

"Over here!" Max yelled. "Look out!"

His warning was too late and Clint felt a bullet nick him across the back. He grunted in pain and then twisted around in the saddle to see an Indian leaping off his horse with his empty rifle coming down like a club.

Clint threw himself off Duke and the Indian landed on his chest. The Gunsith clawed for his six-gun but the Indian's weight had knocked the air from his chest and momentarily dazed him. Fortunately, Max shot the warrior off him or he'd have been a goner.

"Some help you are!" Max raged, tearing the rifle from Clint's fists as the Gunsmith rolled and tried to use his pistol. Still dazed, he missed twice as the Paiutes charged once more.

"I thought you was a gunfighter!" Max shouted.

Clint gritted his teeth and steadied his aim. With his next three bullets, he shot three Indians to Max's one and then

WINNER TAKE ALL

the surviving Paiutes broke and rode their ponies streaking across the sage.

"We did it!" Max shouted. "We beat them!"

"Of course we did," Clint said, reaching around and feeling blood on his fingers. "How bad am I hit?"

Max just glanced at the wound. "You'll live," he said. "But I don't know about Iron Soldier."

Clint's head snapped up and he saw that the great stallion was almost ready to fall. His head was down close to his knees and he was fighting to say on his feet. One look at the animal told the Gunsmith the entire story. He staggered over to Duke and to his own horror, he discovered that a bullet had punctured the skin bag of water.

"There's still a couple gallons in the lower half," he said, tearing off his Stetson. "Here, put your hat in mine for a double wall and let's try and save him."

"Thank you," Max said. "He's in bad shape."

"Maybe so," Clint said, "but they recover fast if they're not too far gone. He just needs to go slow. I think he's finished for this race."

"Don't be too sure of that," Max growled as Iron Soldier drank deeply. "If that damned railroad train that's following us ever gets here, I can water and grain him good. He'll be like a colt in the morning. Besides, your horse looks pretty sorry himself right now."

"He's worn down but he's in no pain."

"After Iron Soldier drinks his fill, has a feedbag of grain, and a few hours of rest and currying, he'll be ready, too," Max said stubbornly.

The Gunsmith did not agree but decided there was no sense in arguing. Max Holloway's veterinarian would be on the train, and he seemed like the kind of man who would tell Max the truth and end the race for the Iron Soldier.

"I wish you'd never suckered me into this mess," Clint

said, feeling gritty in the eyes and out of sorts. "It was my intention to put Duke in one of those livestock cars and let it take us over to the Sierras. This country shouldn't be crossed in the summertime."

Max unsaddled the Iron Soldier. It was clear that he intended to wait for the train, no matter how long it took, because even he could see that the stallion was not fit to ride in its present condition. "If it's too damn tough for you, then quit! Me, I'm pushing on in the morning even if I have to lead this horse all the way to Carson City. I won't be stopped and I won't be beaten."

Clint was about to say something but then he heard a lonesome train whistle somewhere out in the falling darkness. "Better late for you than never," he said.

"Where you going?"

Clint mounted Duke. "I'm in this race to the finish, though I think your horse is done for."

"The hell he is!"

"Killing that stallion won't win the hearts of America to your side," Clint reminded the man. "You want to be a frontier hero, isn't that right?"

"Go to hell!" Max snapped. "You better keep looking over your shoulder, because I'll be there soon!"

Clint rode on down the tracks. The nighttime was the best time to cross the desert. He figured to ride until midnight, sleep for about three hours, then get up and push on. With luck, he would be crossing the border into Nevada by midday tomorrow. He could follow the Humboldt River west, just like so many Forty-Niners had done years ago.

All he had to worry about was rattlesnakes, Indians, scorpions, bad water, not enough water, and the damned sun drying him and Duke up like a split gourd.

TWENTY

Max sat on the hot rails and waited for the train to arrive. He had never felt so dejected in his life and yet, he knew that he would somehow find a way to win the race. But for now, Iron Soldier was finished and, had it not been for his ace-in-the-hole, his "ringer" stallion, things would have been bleak. As it stood, he had a fresh horse. Not a terribly fast horse, but out here in this country and under these conditions, it had become evident to him that speed was secondary to stamina.

As the train neared, Max made up his mind that he would switch horses within a few hours and then go on. He had no doubt that he could overtake the Gunsmith on a fresh horse and pass the man. He would ride his ringer horse as far and as fast as it would go, then he'd have Iron Soldier rested and ready in reserve to push on the last critical miles. Iron Soldiers would be fresh and Clint's gelding would be finished.

The train was moving slow and when its headlight caught Iron Soldier and Max beside the tracks, it creaked to a standstill. Max wasted no time in getting his poor stallion on back toward the livestock cars. In the darkness, it was easy to grab two of his men and issue a terse order. "Let's switch 'em and do it fast! I want to be ready to ride out at midnight."

"After being penned up with all these damn cows since Cheyenne, this boy is ready to run," the cowboy who had been assigned to guard the ringer horse grunted. "Iron Soldier is in bad shape."

Max didn't want to talk about it. He and the cowboys pushed into the livestock car past the cattle. There was a special ramp and, fortunately, it was on the off-side from the dead Indians so they were able to run the ringer horse out and put Iron Soldier away.

"Get this charcoal off of him in a hurry and switch my saddles and gear!" Max grunted. "Bring him up when he's ready and then you get the doc back here to take care of Iron Soldier. I want him ready in case I need him in Reno."

The cowboys exchanged worried glances and it was obvious that they thought Iron Soldier might die before long. Max didn't care what they thought. If the stallion was finished, then there was nothing that could be done except hope the ringer stallion was strong and fast enough to finish the race ahead of Duke. He ought to be, he was young and well-rested. Max started back toward the railroad cars. He knew that people would be searching for him to ask questions about the dead Indians, but he was played out and wanted nothing more than to sleep for a few hours. It had been a long, long night and there were a lot more to come before this race was over.

"Max!"

He turned to see Vicki standing on the roadbed. He was tired and needed sleep but something in her voice arrested his full attention. "Vicki. What's the matter? Looking for the Gunsmith? Well, he's somewhere down the line. You see, we had a little Indian trouble here not long ago."

Vicki looked over toward the crowd of newspaper reporters that were crowding around the dead Indians. "What happened?"

"Clint was in trouble so I bailed him out?" Max replied.

"The truth."

Max was too weary to be clever. "All right. I was the one in trouble so he bailed *me* out. But I shot a few of them before they broke and run."

"Are you . . . are you all right?"

"Do you care?"

Vicki looked closely at her ex-husband. He seemed to have aged ten years and yet . . . yet there was the same unbending steel in him that had attracted her. "I think I still do," she said quietly. "Is Clint all right?"

"Yeah. Took a bullet across the shoulder blades but it's nothing that will stop a man like him. Where's your millionaire?"

"He's out there inspecting the dead Indians like all the others."

"How come you aren't with him?"

Vicki raised her chin. "I don't like Indians," she said. "Dead or alive. Besides, I found out he was already married. He has three children."

Max clucked his tongue in mock sympathy. "Too bad. I guess you must have been pretty disappointed. Thought you really had some money this time, didn't you?"

Vicki managed a thin smile, acknowledging that he was right. They understood each other so well because they were very much alike. Right from the beginning, he'd seen that she was intent on having the good things in life and looking for a man to provide them. Right from the beginning, she'd known that Max was capable of filling that part of the bargain. If only he hadn't been so damned possessive and such a tyrant. He'd given her no slack at all. Made her account for every minute and every dollar.

"I need three or four hours of sleep," he said to her. "I'm out on my feet."

"You're behind," she said. "I hear that Iron Soldier is in bad shape."

"He's about to make a miraculous recovery. Me, too. We'll still win. Did you bet on us, or the Gunsmith?"

"You," Vicki said after a long pause. "I've never seen you lose something that you wanted very badly. I figured you'd not start now. You'll find a way to do it, won't you?"

He moved closer to her. He could smell her hair, the old perfume that she always wore, and that he could never quite shake no matter how many women he might hold in the night.

"I could use a trusted friend, Vicki. This is a winner-takes-all and I could use another ace-in-the-hole."

"Who couldn't?" she whispered, moving closer to him, smelling horse and sweat and liking it. "We used to make a team, didn't we?"

"We were unbeatable." Max drew her into his arms and then he crushed her lips with his own. She melted to his chest and he felt his exhaustion fall away.

"I thought you were out on your feet."

He chuckled. "You're a tonic for me. You always were and you always will be. Help me win this one and I'll be famous. The newspapers will make me another Buffalo Bill Cody and Wild Bill Hickok all rolled into one. We'll make the Grand Tour of Europe. Kings and queens will plead for us to be their guests. We'll become rich."

Vicki closed her eyes. There were people around them everywhere and the smell of men and the train and the hot sage this desert night all combined into a heady brew. "Why don't we sneak into your first-class coach and talk about it?" she breathed.

Max was more than ready. Minutes ago he thought that he could not go another hour without food, drink, and sleep. Now, he wanted nothing but this woman. And once he had her again and she was under his spell and they were a team against the Gunsmith, then nothing was left to chance. He could not fail because she was, deep down, as single-minded and as ruthless in her aims as he was in his own. She had

WINNER TAKE ALL 141

lost her dandy little millionaire. She'd probably even screwed him before learning the truth.

Well, they'd both had their disappointments and little setbacks since leaving Cheyenne. But from this moment forth, things were going to be different.

Max led her quickly down the tracks and into his coach. He locked the doors and when she stood before him, he grabbed the front neckline of her dress with both hands and tore it down to her waist.

"I did that the first time, remember?"

Vicki nodded. She licked her lips in anticipation as she remembered how he had taken her so forcefully the very evening they'd met. Right out behind the barn. He'd torn her dress and thrown her down in the dirt and taken her with his pants pulled down to his knees and his boots still on. He'd been that urgent and she still savored the memory of someone wanting her so damn fiercely that they'd had not even bothered to remove their boots.

"Do it the same way," she panted as his mouth covered her breasts and his tongue laved at her nipples until they were hard as rough pebbles.

Max laughed deep down in his throat. He had a bed but he knew that she wanted it hard and fast and uncomfortable. So he pushed her down in the aisle, shoved her dress up to her waist and ripped her underclothing away. Then, he knelt and unbuckled his belt and yanked his pants down to his knees.

Her legs parted and she began to whimper with ancitipation. "Be gentle," she said, even as he knew she wanted him rough.

He pulled her legs apart and slammed his turgid manhood into her and she gasped in pleasure and then she reached around and grabbed his buttocks. Her fingernails bit into his sore flesh and she whispered, "You smell and feel like a stallion! Now act like one!"

"That's my baby!" he said between gritted teeth as he began to piston in and out of her, banging her up and down on the unyielding floor and exciting her into a wild frenzy.

"Harder!" she moaned. "Just take me hard, Max!"

"I always did," he grunted as he worked over her, the toes of his boots trying to gain purchase on the carpet. "I always. . . . did!"

He lost himself in her, feeling his seed come gushing out in torrents and hearing her cries of delight as she quickly reached her own moment of blissful madness.

It was over. They lay on the floor like two sweating animals, coupled, complete.

"You're going to do whatever needs doing to make me famous, make us rich, aren't you?" he said.

She nodded, her fingers moving up and down his back. "Anything short of killing him or his horse, Max. I won't do that. I don't want you to, either."

He smiled. "I don't think I'll have to. But if I do, just never ask. Understand?"

"Yes." She rolled on top of him and her hips began to grind him back into stiffness.

"You could raise the living from the dead," he whispered.

She looked down at him, her face was bathed in sweat and her eyelids fluttered, half-closed as she concentrated on their coupling. "I know," she whispered. "And if it gets very tough out there in the days ahead, you just remember this moment, and nothing will stop you, Max Holloway."

He tightened his hard buttocks and knew that she was right.

TWENTY-ONE

Of all the passengers, Shorty Evans was the only one to realize that his old boss, Max Holloway, had substituted a ringer for Iron Soldier. The moment he'd seen Iron Soldier with his head down and his legs braced outward as he struggled to stand, the ex-broncbuster knew that the great stallion could not continue the race. And so, when Max had announced that he would be riding out at midnight, Shorty had realized that a ringer horse was hidden in the stock cars and would be switched. There was just no other way that Max could go on and Shorty knew the man well enough to realize that Max would never quit. If it wasn't for the ringer, Max would never have allowed Clint to go into the lead. He'd have pulled a gun and opened fire before he'd have watched that happen.

Shorty had spent the last couple hours thinking about how he could turn his secret knowledge into cash. He had no intention of selling Clint Adams out completely, but that didn't mean he couldn't blackmail Max and set himself up with a little nest egg for his last years. Shorty waited to speak to Max until he could wait no longer. When Max was ready to ride and most of the newspaper reporters had already boarded the train, he limped up to the man and his gray stallion. "I think we'd better have us a little talk, Mr. Holloway."

Max peered down at the old, crippled broncbuster. "You made your choice in Cheyenne. So if it's a job you want back, get lost, you broken-down old has-been."

Shorty bristled with anger and humiliation. The insults made him more determined to milk this arrogant sonofabitch for all he could. Shifting his feet on the trackbed and with the sound of the locomotive huffing in his ears, he looked up at the rider and said, "Mr. Holloway, how much is it worth to you if I don't tell all those nosy reporters how you and your men just switched horses?"

Max had been about to rein away but now, he froze in the saddle. A denial started to rise in his throat, but it died stillborn. Shorty was too much of a horseman to fool and he had been Iron Soldier's groom. Of course he knew about the ringer and the old fool was just desperate and vindictive enough to spill that piece of news to the reporters despite the risk of a bullet.

"Did you see us?" he asked, watching the locomotive engineer wave that he was ready to pull out.

"Didn't have to. I've always known about this horse, though you was too smart to ever have 'em within fifty miles of each other until this race."

"I'm a very careful man. I like to cover every angle."

Shorty touched the gray. "He's got to be Iron Soldier's colt. I never saw two horses that looked more alike. Is he fast?"

"Yeah, but not as fast as the Gunsmith's horse." Max leaned forward. "I got a lot of riding to do, so let's cut the small talk. How much is your silence going to cost me?"

"Five thousand dollars," Shorty blurted. He had really not settled on a price and he would have taken a thousand

WINNER TAKE ALL   145

but he was horse trader enough to shoot high and then bargain his price down.

Max laughed and it was not a pleasant sound. "That's more money than I'll win on the bet."

"Maybe, but you'll pay it because you stand to lose a lot more than that if Clint beats you to Carson City."

"How do I know you won't double-cross me when I win?"

"Because I intend to live to spend the five thousand," Shorty said. "Clint is my friend, but I don't reckon a thousand-dollar loss will hurt him much. I need the money a lot more than he does." Shorty hadn't quite put his thoughts into those words, but the moment he said them he knew they were the truth.

Max looked down into the old man's eyes. He tried to judge his expression and even though the locomotive's headlamp was bright, Shorty's face was a mask. "All right," he said. "Five thousand when I win. If I lose, you can say any damn thing you want and it won't matter."

"You better win," Shorty said. "That five thousand is my retirement. I ain't got a dime saved."

"I know," Max said. "You drank it all up. Just keep your mouth shut and when we overtake the Gunsmith, you keep acting like you hate my guts."

Max reached into his pants pocket and pulled out some twenty dollar bills. "In the meantime, here's a little traveling money."

Shorty took the greenbacks that Max pressed into his waiting palm. He felt rotten and yet, he'd been so broke the last few days he hadn't even had enough to eat. This was going to make things a whole lot easier.

Max started to rein his stallion west and then he stopped.

"Does that black gelding have any flaws that you can see, old man?"

"Nope."

"That's what I thought. So unless the Gunsmith gets scalped or makes a mistake. . . ."

"He won't," Shorty said. "You're going to have to beat him."

Max scowled. "That's what I figured. But I did figure out something tonight. I put it to the test twice and I was right both times."

Shorty's curiosity got the better of him. "What's that?"

Max grinned coldly. "It's that we all got our price. You, me, and Vicki. Even the Gunsmith does, only I haven't bothered to find it. You made a wise decision not to tell the reporters, Shorty. A decision that will put big money in your pocket."

"A man is never too old to get smart," Shorty said, unable to look up at the man.

Max rode away. His horse was young and fresh and Shorty watched the powerful animal gallop out of the locomotive headlamp's glare. He calculated that Max would overtake the Gunsmith by noon tomorrow and then leave him in his dust. Max would reach Carson City first, and when he paid up, Shorty figured he'd give Clint half of his blackmail money.

That way, everybody would win. Clint would still be alive, he'd have twenty-five hundred dollars for his own old age and the country would be fooled into thinking it had another real-life hero.

Shorty climbed stiffly on the train as it started to roll toward Elko. Vicki Flowers was waiting for him. "I see you had business with Max. Something I ought to know?"

"I guess we both know who's going to win this race and

we've placed our real bets tonight, huh, gal?"

His answer made her smile. "You're smarter than I thought you were, Shorty. I'm glad. Poor double-crossing women and old men make bad company."

Shorty grunted and pushed by her. He went to the saloon and bought a bottle of rye whiskey. Then, he moved off to be alone with his betrayal and his liquid comfort. He would make everything up to Clint and he was probably saving his friend's life by keeping his mouth shut about the ringer. If Max won, Clint and Duke would live another day.

TWENTY-TWO

The little Central Pacific railroad town of Elko, Nevada, rested in the clear, blue distance. Clint and Duke jogged wearily toward the settlement with nothing more on their mind than to rest for twenty-four hours, then to push on across the Humboldt Sink and the hot stretches of desert that lay between them and Carson City.

By riding steadily, Clint had made good time, but the heat of the afternoons and the fast accumulation of miles were definitely starting to take their toll. Duke was worn down to less than a thousand pounds while his normal weight was between eleven and twelve hundred. A thousand-pound horse was considered a big riding animal out in the West, but Duke was showing his ribs.

"We're going to get you a pail of oats and some fresh bedding for the night," the Gunsmith promised. "And a new set of shoes. Yours are pumb worn down as thin as dimes."

Duke's ears flicked back and forth in answer. Overhead, a buzzard sailed on the air currents and antelope watched them from a safe distance. This was good cattle country, green and with enough water to support some pretty big cattle ranches. Ten years ago, it had all belonged to the Indians and the only whites who saw it were those passing through on their way to California. But since the transcontinental railroad's completion, Clint could see livestock grazing with the wild mustangs that roamed the picturesque Ruby Mountains to the south.

Clint heard a strange sound and twisted around in his saddle. "Well, I'll be damned," he sighed without any enthusiasm, "it looks to me like we still have a horse race."

Less than three miles behind him, he saw Max Holloway on Iron Soldier. They were galloping slowly along the railroad tracks and the special train was about a half mile behind. To Clint's astonishment, Iron Soldier looked good. His head was up high and his mane was flying in the afternoon breeze.

"Damn," Clint grated. "I was hoping they were out of the running and we could take our time the rest of the way. But don't worry, we're still going to get that night's sleep I've been promising."

Clint turned back in his saddle and returned his gaze to Elko. He could see a tall water tower for the locomotive and the usual shacks and shanties scattered all around the outskirts. At this end was an imposing collection of new corrals that would be railroad's stockyards. The last time that Clint had been through Elko, it had been nothing more than a couple of tent saloons, three or four cribs for the "ladies of the night," and a blacksmith and dry goods store that had carried damn little at exorbitant prices.

Clint twisted around in his saddle again and saw that Max was closing fast on him. He touched Duke with his heels and the gelding broke into a gallop. "If we let him beat us into town, the man will probably buy all the grain and burn it so you can't have a bite. He's mean enough to buy up all the horseshoes, too."

Clint let Duke run but when he turned around in the saddle, he saw that he was still being overtaken. "That horse sure runs as if he's made some kind of miraculous recovery," Clint said. "I wonder what that veterinarian of Max's is feeding him that made him recover so fast."

Max caught Duke three miles outside of town and then swept past him as if he were running in quicksand.

The Gunsmith reined his flagging horse to a walk. "There's no sense in this," he said, confused and disappointed that Holloway had been able to pass him so easily. "We'll just take it slow and steady the rest of the way on in."

Max reined into the only livery in town and dismounted practically on the run. To the surprised liveryman, he yelled, "I want to rent every stall and buy every pound of grain and hay you own!"

The livery owner who also doubled as the town's only blacksmith, looked up from his forge and grinned. He was a big man, shirtless and hairy-chested with powerful arms and shoulders. "Which one are you, Holloway or Adams?"

"The man with the money. You interested in that?"

"Damn right I am. Twenty dollars will do jest fine."

"You got it! Take my horse and put him away in your best stall," Max said. He paid the astonished man. "You just remember, I bought you out of hay, grain, and stalls. You understand me?"

"Yes sir!"

Max stomped off toward the nearest saloon. He would leave in the night and be fifteen or twenty miles ahead by the time the Gunsmith realized that he was gone.

Clint arrived a quarter of an hour later. He rode straight up to the only livery in town and dismounted feeling dead on his feet. He knew that he looked terrible and that people had stared at him on the way into town. His clothes were dirty, and the back of his shirt was torn and blood-stained. He had a beard that was gray with dust and both he and Duke were as poor-looking as they could be.

"I want a good stall with fresh bedding," he said to the

WINNER TAKE ALL

powerful looking man who came forward. "Plenty of grain for—"

The man wiped his sweaty hands on his leather apron. "Sorry. Mr. Holloway bought all my feed and rented all my stalls for the night. I know it's a dirty trick, but he paid me cash money."

Clint knuckled the dust out of his eyes. He was in an ill temper and in no mood for this kind of treatment. "I expected this to happen. I even told my horse it might happen. Now, make me wrong."

The blacksmith clenched his hands into big fists. "I can't do it. Twenty dollars is as much as I make in a month out here. Sorry."

Clint watched Max disappear into a saloon before he returned his attention to the blacksmith. "I guess this is probably the only livery in Elko. That right?"

"Sure is." The man was grinning. He wasn't sorry at all. "Too bad."

Clint dropped his reins and half turned, then he spun around, his gun coming up neat and quick. "I think we'll just march inside. While I rest and my horse eats your oats and hay, you're going to put a fresh set of shoes on him."

The blacksmith looked down at the gun pointed at his belly and his face grew red with anger. Clint saw his knuckles go white and said, "Use your head man! What good is money if you're dead?"

The blacksmith relaxed and then he spun around and marched inside. "Tie him over there in the corner," he spat, going to get oats, hay, and his farrier's box.

Clint tied the horse and then eased his weary body down on a pile of straw. He kept the gun trained on the man while he fed Duke and yanked his old shoes off, grunting, "I'm surprised your horse didn't go lame. These shoes are almost worn through."

"I know. Do a good job and I'll pay you an extra dollar."

The blacksmith growled something that Clint could not understand. He went to his forge and got it hot, then he went to work with a vengence.

Clint nodded off to sleep on the last hoof. He couldn't help it. The bed of straw felt so good that his head dipped until his chin was resting on his chest. The next thing he knew, he was being jerked to his feet and the blacksmith's big fist was smashing into his jaw and he was skidding across the floor.

The blacksmith grabbed his pistol and tossed it into a pile of hay. "You gunfighters are women without a pistol in your hands, aren't you!"

Clint managed to duck a roundhouse swing that would have knocked him out cold. He backed up, trying to make his rubbery legs work. "I don't see any need for this," he said, trying to speak clearly despite the fact that the entire left side of his face seemed to have lost all feeling.

The blacksmith charged and Clint jumped sideways but not fast enough. The man grabbed him and threw him up against a stall. Clint pushed away from it and drove a hard uppercut into the blacksmith's stomach that bounced off without any damage at all. "Maybe we ought to talk our differences out," he suggested.

The blacksmith lunged at him and Clint managed to hammer the man in the ribs before he danced away clean. When the blacksmith roared and charged him again, Clint kicked him right between the legs.

"Ahhh!" the man bellowed and Clint kicked him again. The blacksmith's face lost its color and Clint dived into the hay hunting for his six-gun. He found it just as the blacksmith came staggering forward, blood in his eyes, and murder in his heart.

WINNER TAKE ALL

"Hold it right there! Fun and games are over, mister. One more step and I'll shoot off what I haven't kicked off. Savvy?"

The blacksmith grabbed his crotch. He looked to be in agony but there was still some fight left in him. "Damn you!" he choked.

"I know," Clint said. "It wasn't a fair fight and, if it had been, you'd have won. But life is never fair. So finish up that last shoe and let's part company without any real blood being shed."

The blacksmith finished his work. His face was gray with pain and he could barely bend over to pick up the last hoof. But Clint was not in a sympathetic mood. "After you, I'm going to pay a little visit to Max Holloway and make sure that this kind of thing doesn't happen again," he said.

The blacksmith said nothing but his eyes were filled with so much hatred that Clint added, "Tell you what, I think I'll take some hay and grain along with me instead of leaving my horse behind. He won't mind spending the night outdoors. And somehow, I'll feel a whole lot easier about seeing him in the morning."

Clint took a full thirty pounds of oats and tied it to his saddlehorn, then he took an armful of hay, but he never took his gun off the blacksmith. "So long," he said, heading outside just in time to see the train unloading.

Shorty and Vicki came running to meet him along with a swarm of newspaper reporters. "What happened to you!" Vicki said. "Your face is swelling up on one side."

Clint gave her a lopsided grin. "I fell off my horse."

"Here," Shorty said, taking the hay and Duke's reins. "I'll watch over him while you go get something to eat and find a place to sleep."

"Thanks," Clint said. "See that Duke is curried and do

what you can for him. Iron Soldier passed us on the way in. He seems to be getting stronger by the mile. I don't understand it."

Shorty said nothing as he led Duke through the crowd of reporters who surrounded Clint and fired questions at him from all sides. "Mr. Adams. It appears that it's going to be a neck and neck race across Nevada. Is that your assessment of things?"

Clint looked at the newspapermen. "We got a horse race again," he said.

"Do you still expect to win?"

"I do."

"But how can you? Mr. holloway has men, money, and he seems to be getting stronger as the race goes on. You, well, you look bushed."

Clint shrugged his shoulders. "My horse and I do best when the going gets tough."

The newspapermen liked that kind of spirit and they all scribbled the words down to telegraph east and west. Clint did not care one way or the other. "Vicki," he said. "Have you switched camps on me?"

She took a deep breath and let it out slowly. "I just think you ought to stop this madness and let Max go on and win."

Clint rubbed his jaw and felt the stubble of his beard. "I'll remember your advice," he said, walking away from her and thinking that he would shave and bathe before eating and sleeping. And buy clean clothes. Yes, that would make him feel better.

"Clint!"

He didn't stop walking when she called his name again. He could tell by looking at her face that she had switched her allegiance to Max Holloway and the Iron Soldier. Perhaps he should have expected as much. After all, she had gone after the millionaire publisher and so it was pretty obvious that she was out for what she could get for herself.

The hell with it, Clint thought. The Comstock Lode was just a few miles east of Carson City and there were a lot of pretty women there. He'd find one, just as soon as he collected his ten-thousand dollars in winnings. But right now, he was going to have a few choice words with Max Holloway.

TWENTY-THREE

Clint was steaming when he marched into the saloon and saw Max Holloway holding court with about twenty newspapermen. The moment he stepped inside, all conversation died and the newspapermen fell back from Holloway, who raised a glass in greeting.

"Adams, too bad about your horse having to go without grain. But there's plenty of grass on the outskirts of town. In a couple of days, that gelding will be as frisky as a colt again."

Clint walked slowly across the saloon. From the corners of his eyes he could see that Max had posted several of his men along the walls and there was little doubt that they were ordered to kill him if he made a move for his six-gun. But the saloon was packed with newspaper men, too, and Clint did not think that Holloway really wanted gun trouble.

Holloway's next words confirmed this suspicion when the man said, "Bartender, I want to buy this man a drink of your best whiskey. Clint Adams put up a hell of a good race, but it's over. Anyone who has eyes can see by his face and his horse's ribs that it is."

Clint said nothing. But when the bartender poured him a drink, he raised his glass, smiled, then tossed it in the man's grinning face. Then, very deliberately, he drew the flat of

WINNER TAKE ALL

his hand back and slapped Max Holloway so hard that his head rocked back and blood trickled from his lips. "Sorry about that," he said, raising his eyebrows. "I don't suppose you want to do something about it, though, do you?"

Holloway flushed with humiliation. His right hand slipped down toward his gun butt, fingers twitching with the need to draw. But it would have been suicide. Sure, his men would kill the Gunsmith, but he'd not be alive to see it. Worse yet, Max could hear the pencils scratching, and he knew that he had to do or say something to save face. American heroes did not allow themselves to be slapped like naughty children.

"You're worn down and beaten, Gunsmith. I forgive you for that because even I have tasted the bitter bile of defeat. And since I realize you don't even have the thousand dollars wager you made, I'll also forgive that debt."

"The hell you say," Clint growled, realizing that the man had smoothly managed to turn the tables and make himself look noble instead of just cowardly. Clint had to hand it to this Cheyenne rancher, the man was as slick as cow slobber.

The Gunsmith said, "I'm going to beat you to Carson City and since that apparently means cutting across country and getting away from your railroad side-show, then that's what I figure to do."

If Clint had wanted to shock Max Holloway, he could not have found a better way. The man blinked with surprise, tossed a drink down, and said, "Now wait a minute! You can't do that!"

Clint knew that he had Max where he wanted him. Pouring himself a drink from Max's bottle, he drank it neat and said, "I can and I will. Nothing was ever said about following the transcontinental railroad all the way to Reno. You and the press just made that assumption. But I never did."

"If you leave the rails, you leave the towns and settlements, leave the sure water and protection of the train."

"That's right," Clint said. "I'm leaving all safety and comfort behind. I'm cutting right across Indian lands and desert and saving myself a good hundred miles."

"Are you crazy? You'll get your damned scalp lifted. That six-gun you're so fast with isn't going to save your life and neither is your rifle if you get jumped by a pack of Paiutes."

Clint just shrugged his shoulders as if he hadn't a care in the world. Never mind that he was out on his feet and so was Duke. Tomorrow was a new day and things had to improve. "It's a big country out there and maybe they aren't all on the prod," Clint said. "I can make sign language. I'll get a few trinkets to trade and I already have a skin water bag. There's things to shoot and eat. Rattlesnakes are good and a man can go a long ways on a sack of lizards."

"Lizards!" Max looked disgusted and several of the newspaper reporters just shook their heads in amazement.

"A frontiersman can do what he has to do," Clint said, speaking more to the reporters than to his competitor. "I've been around Apache down in Arizona who would think the worst part of Nevada was paradise. I can find water and feed for my horse, too. A real frontiersman learns those things. Many are the times that I've chased outlaws into the badlands with nothing to eat or drink for days."

"Don't listen to him!" Max shouted, hearing the pencils scratch.

But it was too late. Suddenly, the interest had swung back to the Gunsmith, and though his natural modest instincts were to avoid talking about himself, he knew that elaborating on about a few of more exciting exploits was just the thing that would goad Max Holloway into saying

WINNER TAKE ALL

something stupid or desperate. Something that would show him in his true light.

"I remember the time I was hunting Geronimo down near the Mexican border," he was saying. "We had not had a drink in five days and—"

"That's impossible!" Max shouted. "An outrageous lie. Don't any of you newspaper men believe that. A person cannot get by without water in the desert for more than seventy-two hours before he either dies or cannot function."

"That may be true," Clint said. "But not if he knows how to find the leaves of the Ki-yack-yack tree."

"The what!"

"The Ki-yack-yack tree," Clint repeated very patiently as if explaining it to a small boy. "It's an Apache word for a 'water-and-nectar-giving tree that grows well in the desert.' I would have expected an old Pony Express hero like yourself to have known that."

"The Pony Express ran about five hundred miles north of Arizona!" Max snorted. "Furthermore, I'm sure that your old Apache experiences are of no interest to these men and that—"

"Just a minute, Mr. Holloway," Bobby Bouchard interrupted. "We've heard a lot from you all the way from Cheyenne. But very little is known about the Gunsmith's remarkable past. I think I, and the rest of the reporters would like to hear more before he strikes courageously across the wastelands of Nevada."

The other journalists were in total agreement. Clint beamed. Max Holloway grew absolutely livid and stomped out of the saloon.

Clint had all the drinks he wanted as he took a chair and put his feet up on the table. Then, with a crowd of newspapermen surrounding him, he started to spin some of the grandest tales ever heard on the frontier. Tales as wild and impossible as the dime novels that had often been written about him, Cody, Hickok, and the others.

Throughout the long evening, pencils were scratching.

At midnight, he went up to a room and went to bed, little drunk and very pleased with himself. He slept until noon feeling much better than he had since leaving Cheyenne. He bathed, went to the general store, and bought new clothes and Indian trinkets he hoped would save his bacon if he got in a fix with them. Then, Clint had a shave before eating a huge breakfast.

He was just finishing up his third cup of coffee when Max Holloway stomped into the cafe and shouted, "Goddammit, when are you riding out?"

Clint looked up at the man. Sixteen hours ago, Max had beat him into town and had looked a sure winner. Now, the man appeared haggard and out of sorts. Max Holloway looked anything but confident.

"Why do you ask?" Clint said, knowing the answer. "I would have thought you and the train would have been long gone by now. You know, you really do need a headstart since you'll be going so much farther than Duke and I."

"Cut the shit! I'm sticking with you all the way to the outskirts of Carson City and then I'll make you eat my dust."

Clint frowned. "I don't remember extending an invitation."

Max would have killed this man if he could have and a hero's image be damned. Clint had blown all his plans to switch back to the real Iron Soldier in Reno to make the final sprint down to Carson City on a fresh horse. Now, Max knew he had no choice but to either go with Iron Soldier who had not totally recovered, or to stick with his ringer. He had been up all night weighing the tough choice and finally, he'd decided to go with his ringer. The horse was young, strong, and ready. Iron Soldier was old, sick, and too valuable to ruin in what would be a mad race across hell.

"Well," Clint asked with a look of dry amusement. "Did I invite you along?"

"No, but it's a free country, isn't it?"

Clint weighed the statement. He was not opposed to Max Holloway coming along. It would be just the two of them without Max's hired men to complicate things. "Yeah, I guess it is. All right," he said. "You can come along."

"Gee," Max said with dripping sarcasm, "what a treat."

Clint finished his coffee and paid his bill. He went outside and was met by a throng of reporters begging him to continue where he had left off the night before.

"Sorry," he told them. "But storytime is over and I've a race to win. By the way, Max here has asked me if I would show him the way across the Nevada wilderness."

"Why would you do that?" a reporter shouted.

"Because I believe in fair play," Clint said poker-faced. He heard Max choke with pent-up rage but the man said nothing. "So I have agreed."

"What a sport," a reporter gushed with admiration.

Vicki pushed her way through the crowd. She took one look at Max and seemed to read his dark thoughts. Before he left with the Gunsmith, she would remind him of his promise not to kill either the Gunsmith or Duke. But when their eyes met, she saw something inside of him that told her that Max would not be held to any such promise.

Max was fit to kill.

TWENTY-FOUR

They rode out of Elko side by side waving good-bye to a crowd of disgruntled newspapermen who suddenly found themselves with nothing to write about. There was no doubt about it now, the train would make haste to Reno and the newspapermen would hurry down to Carson City to be waiting for Clint and Max to cross the finish line. They weren't happy about the arrangement, but there was nothing they could do about it. The die was cast.

To Max's way of thinking, the entire idea of cutting across country was both dangerous and stupid. If they intended to stay together anyway, then why not follow the railroad tracks and wait until the last and then make a sprint for Carson City? At least that way they would have a guarantee of food, water, and some protection from the train.

Max had tried to explain to the Gunsmith how crazy it was to go across Nevada, but the ex-lawman's mind was set and there was no doubt that he intended to do things his way. "You do what you think will work best," Clint said, "because that's what I'm going to do."

"What kind of a horse race is this with no one watching!" Max cried in anger and frustration.

"A better one. Now, it'll just be the two of us. The best

WINNER TAKE ALL

man and the best horse will win. No tricks, no funny games with any of your men. If you attempt to kill me or my horse, I'll kill you first. I like it simple like that."

Max studied the black gelding. He was furious and he wanted to undermine the Gunsmith's confidence. "He doesn't look like the same horse as when we left Cheyenne."

"Neither does that gray," Clint replied, his voice taking on a cutting edge. "Did you switch on me?"

Max felt his heart clog his throat. "Hell no! What the devil are you talking about?" Max demanded, summoning up as much outrage as he could muster.

"It's been done before," Clint said. "But if that's a different stallion, he's a dead ringer. The best I ever saw."

"It's the Iron Soldier, make no mistake about that," Max lied. "Besides, if I'd have switched, don't you think old Shorty Evans would have been the first to notice? After all, he was my groom and horse handler."

"That occured to me," Clint said. "In fact, that's the only reason I didn't bring the subject up in Elko. If you'd switched, Shorty would have noticed it right away. But the thing of it is, this horse looks too fresh, and he and Duke don't want to fight the way they did before."

"That's because your gelding is on his last legs," Max said as he touched spurs to his stallion and let the animal gallop. He had expected the Gunsmith to match his pace, but when he looked over his shoulder, Clint Adams was still jogging along nice and easy. Max built a two-mile lead and then he reined his horse in. Who was he kidding? Only a fool would ride off alone while crossing the heart of Paiute country.

"Damn him!" Max swore aloud. "He's got me one to one and he knows I won't leave him and his guns behind."

• • •

The country had grown far more desolate as they moved southwest. Max had never seen such a wasteland. As far as the eye could see, there was little except sage, rotting mountain ranges with almost no trees, and rocks. Now and then, they'd come across a small stream and for two days, they rode without any water except for what they carried. Max was glad that he had taken Clint's lead and bought himself a large skin bag and a Winchester before leaving Elko. But even so, it was not enough to satisfy their thirsts. A hot horse could drink five or six gallons at a time.

"I don't know how you keep finding these water holes when we seem to be most desperate," he remarked one blazing afternoon. "But I sure am glad you can."

Clint surveyed the hot desert floor. "I follow the mustang tracks," he said absently. "Wild horses pretty much go from one water hole to the next in this country. And if I don't see any of their tracks, then I watch for birds and other wild animals."

"No Ki-yack-yack trees out here?"

Clint had a smile. "Too far north," he said.

"How far are we from Carson City?"

Clint shrugged. "How should I know? I've never been this way before."

"Well, you must have some idea!"

"I do."

"Well?"

"About seventy miles is all. You see that alkaline valley out there?"

"Yeah."

"Well I think that is what they call the Carson Sink. It's where the Carson River has sunk into the desert. Just beyond those low hills we should find the tag end of the river. As we follow it west, there will be plenty of trees, grass, and

WINNER TAKE ALL 165

water to lead us right into Carson City."

Max was surprised and almost overcome with joy. "That's . . . that's wonderful. We can be there by tomorrow evening!"

"Not in this heat." Clint wiped his brow with his sleeve. The sun was a torment and the land seemed to undulate with heat waves.

Max fell into a brooding silence. He thought his horse had the strength to push across these last few miles and he was about ready to leave the Gunsmith behind now that he knew that he could find his way to Carson City.

That night, with the moon out full and the stars shining brilliantly, they crossed the alkali flats. It was eerie. The alkali was about three inches deep and cracked, and as white as dried milk spilled across a tabletop. It crunched when the horse's hooves broke through and then little puffs of white powder lifted up behind them to hang like two smoke trails in the moonlight. The flats were about seven miles across and nothing lived on them although you could see that the flats were flooded each spring with the Sierra snow runoff. But now, they were criss-crossed with the trails of unshod Indian ponies.

"I don't understand what the Paiutes are upset about," Max groused just as the sun was coming up. "This land isn't worth anything anyway."

"It's all they have," Clint said. "The problem is, these people had things hard enough before the white men came. Mostly, they lived off the pinion pine nuts that once covered this land. But when gold and silver were discovered in Virginia City and across those mountains up ahead, miners by the thousands poured over the Sierras from California's played-out strikes. The first thing they did was cut down the pinion pines and either use them for firewood or underground shoring. So the Paiutes began to get real hungry and mean when the trees that they'd been harvesting for centuries were falling by the thousands."

"The hell with them!" Max growled. "The best Indians are dead Indians. The sooner we either kill or starve them off this continent, the better."

Clint shook his head. "I'm afraid that's pretty much the sentiment of the military generals that oversee the forts out West. Congress isn't much more sympathetic."

"What are you, some damned Indian-lover? Have you already forgotten how they tried to kill us back in Wyoming?"

"Of course not. And when the arrows started flying, I fought for my life—and yours. But I don't hate Indians. They're just fighting for their own existence the same as the rest of us."

"You sound like a damned Bible-thumper," Max said with disgust.

Clint clamped his jaws in silence and rode on through a spectacular sunrise. When they finally jogged off the alkali flats and topped a long bench and then a series of low mountains, they reined their horses in and sat in silence as they studied the panorama before them. Each man was grateful for the sight in his own way. They could see the Carson River winding out of the eastern Sierra foothills. The river was clogged with heavy stands of cottonwood trees as it meandered off the mountains then ran lazily toward them. The cottonwoods were so thickly bunched that they almost obscured the river itself from view. With the rising sun warming their backs, the water shone like bars of silver. After riding for hundreds of miles across nothing but sagebrush, the glistening Carson River and the cottonwood groves were beautiful.

"Where, exactly, is Carson City?" Max asked.

WINNER TAKE ALL 167

"We follow the river and it runs within a couple miles east of town. Easy to find."

"That's all I wanted to know," Max said, tightening down his Stetson and whipping his gray stallion. "I'll see you in Carson City. Have your money ready!"

Clint started after him. He let Duke break into a gallop but he did not allow the gelding free rein. Carson City was still a good twenty miles to the west and that was too damned far to ask a horse to run after the grueling days that they'd already endured. Clint would not allow Duke to kill himself in a headlong race across these final miles.

But Max obviously did not share his concern. The man swept off the brushy hill and headed straight for the river. Clint saw him extend his lead to a mile, then two miles, but just as Max was about to disappear over a low set of hills, something caught the Gunsmith's eye.

He blinked and squinted and then he saw at least twenty mounted Indians come streaming over the hills and block Max's escape toward Carson City. Iron Soldier veered sharply toward the river and Clint could hear the distant popping of gunfire. He saw Max and then the Indians disappear into the cottonwood groves for almost a full minute then come flying out with the Indians still on his tail.

Clint swore. The bastard was leading the Paiute warriors right straight back to him! The Gunsmith reined Duke toward a place farther down river by at least two miles. Max would have to follow him if he stood any chance of survival and they would both have to find a place to make a good stand beside the water. It was their only hope; caught out in the sage, the Indians would pick them off or flank them and the end would come swiftly.

Duke seemed to understand. He was played out but game and now, he laid his ears back and raced to save the

Gunsmith's life. Clint could hear Max shouting his name, but there was no time to look back. The cottonwoods were coming up fast and the Gunsmith knew that he had to find a low bluff or a riverbank or something to cover his back.

Clint reached the cover of trees in a hail of bullets and arrows. He raced wildly downriver giving Duke his head and letting the gelding pick his own trail. They jumped over fallen trees, swerving wildly through places that no horse should ever run. A profusion of low branches whipped Clints's face and tore his Stetson from his head. He knew that he had to find a defensible position soon because the river was petering out fast. In another mile or two, the trees would thin out as the water bled into the sandy earth and then their precious cover would be completely gone.

"Wait for me!" Max shouted. "Wait, dammit!"

Clint swung around in the saddle and saw Max charging after him. But just as he was about to turn back around, a low branch caught the Gunsmith across the side of his head and raked him out of the saddle. Clint struck a blanket of dead leaves and rolled. He was on his feet, dazed and wobbly, but fully awake.

Max was going to run him down! The man did not even slow his horse until Clint drew his six-gun and aimed at his chest in a gesture that left no doubt whatsoever as to his intentions—stop and pick me up or I'll shoot you right out of the saddle. For an instant, time seemed to stand still and then Max yanked on the reins. He threw out his arm and Clint jumped. Their hands slapped together like a shot and the stallion's forward momentum whipped Clint off the ground. For a terrifying instant, it seemed as if Max would be torn out of his saddle and that they would both crash to the earth. Max had no saddlehorn to hang onto, so he grabbed the stallion's mane with his right hand and, somehow, they both managed to stay mounted as the stallion thundered downriver after Duke.

Clint twisted around and opened fire on the pursuing Indian warriors. Their leader flipped over backward off his pony but the others were coming hard, even madder now that one of their own had been the first to die.

Carson City had never seemed farther away.

TWENTY-FIVE

Their train had steamed into Reno and the crowd of journalists had dispersed, some to the telegraph office, others like Vicki and Shorty, rushed straight for the stageline that would deliver them to Carson City. Now, as they bounced along the dusty road toward Carson City, Shorty pulled a bottle of whiskey out of his saddlebags and began to drink in brooding silence. Every once in a while, he would look up accusingly at Vicki and his stare made her squirm. "You should stop drinking so much," she said when they finally reached the territorial capitol. "You'll kill yourself with that stuff."

"It don't matter anymore," he said. "Without honor, what the hell is life worth? Have you asked yourself that one yet, Miss Flowers?"

Vicki flushed with embarrassment and hurried away, hearing the drunken old man yell, "We're a couple of Judas's, that's what we are!"

A journalist who had vaulted out of the stagecoach even before it had stopped rolling, now came rushing back. "We beat them!" he shouted. "Holloway and the Gunsmith haven't arrived yet."

The man's peers hooted with relief despite the fact that logic dictated that the train, even though its route was a

WINNER TAKE ALL

hundred miles longer, would still arrive in Reno at least a day ahead of the horse racers.

"They should be here this afternoon or tonight," a cowboy drawled as the reporters turned to him, eager for a local's advice. "I rode that way once. 'Course, there wasn't any Indian war going on then, but I did it."

"Have you been following this race?"

"Hell yes!" the cowboy said with indignation. "The whole damn territory is betting on this race. Why, up on the Comstock Lode, the odds-makers have it dead even—if the Indians don't scalp 'em along the way."

Vicki shivered at the prospect, and Shorty Evans just raised his bottle of whiskey at the sky and glared redly at her. She did not like the old man, and she was afraid he was going to make trouble for her if he kept drinking. If he started talking and revealed that Max had switched horses at Elko, then things were going to fall apart in a hell of a hurry. The press would jump on that kind of a scandal and they'd sniff out the truth like a pack of bird dogs. Vicki knew she had to have a talk with Shorty before it was too late.

"The Ormsby House is filled up," Bobby Bouchard said, taking her arm, "but money talks and I think I can find us accomodations."

"Go to hell!" she snapped, pulling her arm away. "Or better yet, go back to your wife and grow up to be a man."

His cheeks flamed, and several men who had overheard his crude proposition snickered. Bouchard stomped away and Vicki knew that she had just passed up a chance to make a lot of money. To hell with it. She'd stick with Max Holloway because the Gunsmith sure would never trust her again.

Vicki found a room in a small boarding house on Robinson Street. She did not expect to spend more than twenty-four hours there, believing that Clint and Max would arrive at any minute. And like everyone else, she prepared for their arrival by packing some food and drink and then going out to the east end of town and waiting near the Carson River. She'd be damned if she was going to sleep through the finish.

There were at least a thousand spectators that spent the night on the desert. Fortunately, the weather was warm and the moon was almost full. Every few hours, some overanxious fool would shout that he saw riders on the eastern skyline. At that point, everyone would jump up and crane their necks to see Clint and Max come bursting out of the semi-darkness and race neck and neck for the city. But it was always a false alarm and, by daybreak, the crowd had grown irritable and impatient. Some people packed up their blankets and food and returned to the town. Others napped. The day grew hotter and hotter and they all took shade under the cottonwood trees. Men jumped in the river and women waded with their skirts held modestly in their hands so that they could cool their feet and ankles. By late afternoon less than a hundred spectators remained, half of them dead drunk.

Shorty Evans staggered over to Vicki and crashed into the sage; she hoped he would just pass out and leave her in silence. But he did not.

"You're a Judas, admit it," he said in a slurred voice. "We both are."

"We're both realists," she said to him. "Listen, we know about the ringer horse and that it will give Max the edge. And maybe we did wrong, but it's done. You took money, I made bets on the Iron Soldier. There's no going back, so why don't you keep your loose mouth shut and be content with the money?"

Shorty pushed himself around and sat cross-legged in the brush, his face ruined, his eyes tortured with guilt and whiskey. "Money ain't worth it," he said. "Not to betray a friend."

"It's done!" she hissed. "If it's killing you so much, then confess to Clint and give Max whatever he paid you back. But keep quiet or you're liable to get yourself—and Clint—shot!"

Shorty nodded. Even drunk, he knew that she was right. Besides, he would split the winnings with Clint. And that made it all right, didn't it?

By the third evening, only a few spectators lay scattered under the cottonwood trees. Even the most dedicated journalists had gone back into Carson City to stay in the hotel and the saloons. Many were composing obituaries for both Max Holloway and Clint Adams. No one was betting on a horse race anymore, but instead, they were laying wagers on whether or not the pair were alive. The odds were heavily in the opinion that they were both lying out in the desert pincushioned with arrows and missing their scalps.

Shorty came back to Vicki's blanket. They were both haggard. Neither had slept, bathed, or eaten anything approaching a solid meal. "What do you want now, to purge your conscience again?" she asked, too exhausted and dispirited to summon up any real anger toward the pathetic old man.

"You've got some money, don't you?"

She looked him in the eye. "I won't give you any to buy whiskey."

He drew himself up. "I want to rent a livery horse. I'm going to go find them."

Vicki blinked. "That's insane. You heard the sheriff. The army is sending help but until then, it would be crazy to follow the Carson River east. That country is alive with Paiutes."

"I don't give a damn. I got to live with myself. You got to do the same. It's the only way."

Vicki drew her knees up under her chin. She was also going crazy waiting and wondering if Clint and Max were dead or alive. "You're saying we should disobey the sheriff's orders, rent horses, and go find them?"

"That's right. And if you won't help, then I'm going to steal a horse and a rifle and go alone. I just figured since you betrayed the Gunsmith the same as me, that you'd want to do something to square things."

Vicki took a deep breath and expelled it slowly. She had been fantasizing about just such a bold action. But fantasy could not take the place of cold reality. Vicki had heard stories about what Indian braves did to young white women, and they were enough to chill her blood.

"We could stay near the trees and cover," Shorty said, seeming to read her fears. "If you have enough money, I found two damn fast horses. Both of 'em could easily outrun any Indian ponies. I know horses. I know what I'm talking about."

She frowned. "Max said that, if they came across any Indians, he and the Gunsmith could outrun them. And yet, look what's happened."

"That's different," Max said stubbornly. "Their horses were played out. We'd be on fresh ones."

Vicki closed her eyes. She was truly frightened. But at the same time, she owed the Gunsmith, and Max did love her. "All right. I'll get you the money and you get everything we need. But no whiskey!"

The old broncbuster nodded. "You got my word on it!"

They rode out alone, just about midnight. As they passed through the few spectators who would not give up or else had nothing better in life to do than to wait indefinitely, several of them called out to come back. But Vicki ignored their advice and rode on, keeping just north of the dark line of river and trees. She was more afraid now that she was actually doing what she knew was right than she had ever been in her life, but also more determined. Always before, she'd done the easiest thing, the thing that would stand the best chance of making her rich. Now, she was finally doing the right thing. So she felt scared, but also very good.

"How would we find their . . . their bodies in the dark?" she asked the old man who rode beside her.

Shorty's face was hard. He had not had a drink in the last six hours and his hands were shaking so bad he had to hang onto the saddlehorn. If he needed to use a gun, he would not be able to hit anything but it was best not tell the woman. "If they're dead, we'll either hear coyotes fighting to strip their bones, or see buzzards in the morning—or we might just smell 'em."

Vicki tried to swallow and couldn't. She shivered with dread and pushed the image of Clint and Max from her mind. "I think they're alive," she said, knowing that she sounded desperate and childish. "I just can't see them both dead. Not on their fast horses. Can you?"

Shorty said nothing. He was hung over and sick to his stomach. He needed a drink so bad that it was all he could do to keep from turning his horse around and riding back to a saloon in Carson City. But he couldn't do that and not put a bullet through his own head, so he was trapped into riding on.

"Shorty?"

"What!" he snapped, not wanting to talk.

"What happened to you? Why did you turn to the bottle?"

"I got old and afraid," he said with bitterness. "It'll happen to you, too. It happens to everyone."

Vicki did not agree. It might happen to people who found themselves old, homeless, and poor. But not to old people who had money. She'd seen rich old men and women, they didn't look afraid, but maybe it was easier to hide your fears when you were rich.

They rode on and on, sometimes galloping when they found a good trail, but mostly just walking through the sage, Shorty in the lead, Vicki following and eating his dust.

Daylight found them about fifteen miles east of town, alone and in a country that seemed abnormally silent.

Shorty got down and relieved himself, not even bothering to turn his back to Vicki who turned her head and stared back the way they had come. The sunrise was hot and burned directly into their eyes. There wasn't a breath of air and the dead land seemed to be waiting for something bad to happen.

And it did. Suddenly, just ahead they heard an explosion of gunfire and then the screams of Indian warriors attacking.

Vicki's heart stopped. She whirled her horse around and then she whipped it into a run. Behind her, she heard Shorty yell for her to stop.

But Vicki didn't listen. She raced away, mindless with panic, and when her racing horse stepped in a hole and somersaulted her into the air, she screamed—not in fear of her landing or being landed upon, but in abject terror of being caught afoot by a pack of wild Indians bent on torture and rape.

TWENTY-SIX

Clint and Max had held the Indians off for two days, and they were running low on ammunition. Much too low to survive another day.

"It'll be daylight in a few minutes," Clint said, tightening his cinch and checking his gun. "I've got six bullets left in my gun and nothing left in my Winchester. What about you?"

"Two bullets in my six-gun," Max said grimly. "Nothing left in my rifle. What the hell chance have I got with two bullets?"

Clint ejected two shells from his pistol and gave them to the man. "Now we've got four each. Make them count. Don't open fire until we hit their line and we're right on top of them."

Max stared at the two shells Clint had given him. "I wouldn't give you these if the situation was reversed," he said.

"I know. Mount up and let's get this over with."

They both stepped into the saddle. The gray stallion and Duke were ready to run after a good rest and Clint knew that, if they could just break through the line of Indians, they'd soon outdistance the Paiutes and reach the safety of Carson City.

Dawn was starting to streak across the hills. As they waited in the cottonwood trees for the light to strengthen enough for them to see their way ahead, the sky colored gold and red. It occurred to Clint that he might never see another sunrise. They'd fought well and long here, but yesterday, more Paiutes had arrived and now there were at least thirty, and they had them surrounded. Clint was sure the Paiutes intended to strike early this morning and when they did, they would be successful.

"Ready?" Clint asked.

Max nodded. "I want to say something before we do this."

"Make it fast," Clint told him.

"If I get killed and you live, make sure that Vicki gets my ranch and everything. I wrote it out in that last will and testimony I gave you yesterday."

"I'll do it," Clint said, raising his reins and starting to lean forward in the saddle.

"And if I live," Max added quickly, "I want you to know that you're the best man I ever rode beside. Better than any of the Pony Express boys, even. That's why I've a confession to make before we go."

Clint was filled with growing impatience. This was no time to start confessing things. They needed to run for their lives!

"I'm riding a ringer," Max said. "This stallion is Iron Soldier's son. The Soldier, well, he wasn't recovered enough to go on so I switched horses. So even if you get to Carson City after me, you've still won the race."

Clint was flabbergasted. "You never cease to amaze me! Here we are, poised to run a gauntlet, and you're thinking about that damned winner-take-all horse race. I don't give a damn about that now!"

"Yeah, but you will if we live to see Carson City. And

I knew I would, too. So, right now, I'm making that confession because I probably wouldn't do it if we get out of this alive."

"Well thanks," Clint said, taking the man's hand and shaking it. "Now let's do our best to get out of this mess with our scalps."

"There's no one I'd rather go through this with than you, Gunsmith. And—"

Clint appreciated the confession and the heart-felt compliment but enough was enough so he kicked Duke and the black shot out of the trees, gathering speed and cutting straight at the Indians. Max, caught a little by surprise, recovered and came storming after him, the gray stallion trying its damnedest to overtake the gelding and not succeeding.

The Indians were up and readying for their own attack, but Clint had caught them five or ten minutes early. They weren't mounted yet and by the time they realized that two crazy fools were striking into their lines, it was too late.

Clint shot a brave who jumped into his path and the warrior crashed into the brush. That first bullet seemed to ignite something akin to a Chinese New Year's celebration as the Indians opened fire. Clint hit the Paiute skirmish line leaning over his saddlehorn, using three of his four bullets carefully and making them count. He broke through the Indians and veered Duke to the west, running for Carson City. He was out in the open and running free. Nothing could—

"Clint! My horse!"

Clint twisted around in the saddle just in time to see the ringer stallion fall. Max, being a fine horseman, kicked out of his stirrups and sailed forward. He landed on his feet and started running as, less than four hundred yards behind him, the Paiutes jumped for their own horses. A few just took off running after the horseless white man.

Clint swore and pulled hard on the reins. Duke slid down on his haunches and when he was stopped, Clint spun the black around on his heels and sent him racing back to save Max. He stuck his hand out and pulled Max up behind him, and they galloped west again.

"We'll never make it riding double!" Max shouted.

"Shut up and start shooting!" the Gunsmith ordered.

"I can't. I'm out of bullets."

Clint shoved his gun behind his back and yelled, "There's just one bullet left so make it count!"

Max twisted around on the running horse. He stuck his arm out but Duke was running so hard over such broken land that he knew he'd hit nothing if he pulled the trigger, so he shoved the gun back into Clint's holster and yelled, "Save that one for yourself!"

Clint tried to look back but Max was blocking his view so he just rode as hard as he could, trusting Duke to take them as far as possible and then they'd let the chips fall where they might. He was sure they would be overtaken in a few miles and then knocked off Duke with war axes or else run through with lances.

"Whoo-wee!" Shorty Evans cried as he came racing over a low hill into view.

Clint blinked in disbelief. Had Shorty gone crazy! He wasn't leading any cavalry attack, he was all alone!

Shorty threw a six-gun to Clint and a Winchester to Max before he hauled his own gun out. Clint beckoned toward a hilltop. "We've got to take a stand or they'll cut us down from behind. Let's go up there!"

They barely made the hilltop but when they did, they hunkered down in the rocks and opened fire on the Paiutes with devastating effect. The Indians broke their charge about forty yards from the rocks and retreated. Clint turned to thank Shorty but his grateful words fell silent. Shorty had taken a bullet right through the forehead and died without a sound.

"Damn!" Clint whispered. "Let's get out of here, Max. He died to give us a chance to live. Let's not let it be wasted."

TWENTY-SEVEN

They rode like hell for Carson City, quickly outdistancing the Indians, who finally gave up the chase. When they caught up with Vicki, she was leading her lame horse, tears streaming down her face, gun clenched in her fist.

"I turned and ran when I heard the Indians," she said, looking up at Max and the Gunsmith. "I lost my head and because of it, this horse injured his leg. I haven't even the guts to use my gun and put him out of his misery. I'm a coward."

She drew a ragged berath. "What happened to Shorty?" she said in a small voice.

"He was killed by the Indians after he helped save our lives," Clint said, keeping his eyes on their backtrail in case the Paiutes changed their mind and came back. But they wouldn't. Carson City and the Comstock Lode was too close, and there was no way for them to know that Vicki was afoot and in trouble.

The Gunsmith and Max dismounted and inspected the lame animal. Clint flexed its fetlock and knee. "There's nothing broken. He's probably just pulled something and needs some liniment and rest."

Vicki brightened. "Do you think so?"

"Uh-huh. Max?"

WINNER TAKE ALL

He was studying her closely. "Yeah. Just a sprain, I'd say. Why did you come clear out here, Vicki? A coward would never have left Carson City."

"I still ran."

Max gently touched her face and used his thumb to wipe away her tears. "But you still tried," he said. "That took courage. Was it all just for the Gunsmith, or was part of it for me?"

"For you, too."

Max Holloway took a deep breath and pulled her close. He looked at the Gunsmith and said, "You've won. You ride into Carson City and collect your ten thousand. It's on deposit at the Bank of Nevada. You'll have no trouble. You can tell them what I did but I'd appreciate it if you'd not say where I'm going."

Clint remounted Duke. "Where exactly are you going?"

Max kissed his ex-wife on the forehead and said, "Honey, the Comstock Lode is just a little ways farther. I've always wanted to see Virginia City. Interested in coming along?"

"But what about . . ." she tried to put it all into words. "You know, the reporters, the world tour, fame, and. . . ."

"The hell with it," Max said wearily. "I don't deserve to be famous. I cheated and I still lost. All I want is you to be my wife again. Just like when I had nothing. We were happy then, and I've still got Iron Soldier and a ranch. Even losing the ten thousand, I'm not wanting for anything but you."

She smiled. "Do you really mean that?"

He nodded. "Marry me again. I swear I've changed."

Vicki sniffled. "I believe you have."

Clint said good-bye to them and the last he saw of Vicki Flowers and Max Holloway, they were walking hand in hand leading both their horses up toward the nearby Comstock Lode. The Gunsmith would take his ten thousand dollars in winnings, but he'd say nothing about the dead ringer horse or old Shorty Evans who'd played out his last cards like a man anyone would have been proud to call a friend.

Ten thousand dollars was a lot of money, but as the Gunsmith rode on to Carson City, he knew that he'd give it all away without a thought for the likes of a good old friend like Shorty.

Watch for

MESSAGE FROM A DEAD MAN

eighty-sixth novel in the exciting

GUNSMITH series

coming in February!

J. R. ROBERTS
THE GUNSMITH
SERIES

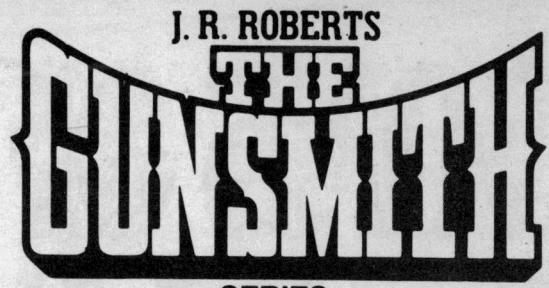

☐ 0-441-30965-8	THE GUNSMITH #61: THE COMSTOCK GOLD FRAUD	$2.50
☐ 0-441-30966-6	THE GUNSMITH #62: BOOM TOWN KILLER	$2.50
☐ 0-441-30967-4	THE GUNSMITH #63: TEXAS TRACKDOWN	$2.50
☐ 0-441-30968-2	THE GUNSMITH #64: THE FAST DRAW LEAGUE	$2.50
☐ 0-441-30969-0	THE GUNSMITH #65: SHOWDOWN IN RIO MALO	$2.50
☐ 0-441-30970-4	THE GUNSMITH #66: OUTLAW TRAIL	$2.75
☐ 0-515-09058-1	THE GUNSMITH #67: HOMESTEADER GUNS	$2.75
☐ 0-515-09118-9	THE GUNSMITH #68: FIVE CARD DEATH	$2.75
☐ 0-515-09176-6	THE GUNSMITH #69: TRAIL DRIVE TO MONTANA	$2.75
☐ 0-515-09217-7	THE GUNSMITH #71: THE OLD WHISTLER GANG	$2.75
☐ 0-515-09329-7	THE GUNSMITH #72: DAUGHTER OF GOLD	$2.75
☐ 0-515-09380-7	THE GUNSMITH #73: APACHE GOLD	$2.75
☐ 0-515-09447-1	THE GUNSMITH #74: PLAINS MURDER	$2.75
☐ 0-515-09493-5	THE GUNSMITH #75: DEADLY MEMORIES	$2.75
☐ 0-515-09523-0	THE GUNSMITH #76: THE NEVADA TIMBER WAR	$2.75
☐ 0-515-09550-8	THE GUNSMITH #77: NEW MEXICO SHOW DOWN	$2.75
☐ 0-515-09587-7	THE GUNSMITH #78: BARBED WIRE AND BULLETS	$2.95
☐ 0-515-09649-0	THE GUNSMITH #79: DEATH EXPRESS	$2.95
☐ 0-515-09685-7	THE GUNSMITH #80: WHEN LEGENDS DIE	$2.95
☐ 0-515-09709-8	THE GUNSMITH #81: SIX GUN JUSTICE	$2.95
☐ 0-515-09760-8	THE GUNSMITH #82: THE MUSTANG HUNTERS	$2.95

Please send the titles I've checked above. Mail orders to:

BERKLEY PUBLISHING GROUP
390 Murray Hill Pkwy., Dept. B
East Rutherford, NJ 07073

NAME_____

ADDRESS_____

CITY_____

STATE_____ZIP_____

Please allow 6 weeks for delivery.
Prices are subject to change without notice.

POSTAGE & HANDLING:
$1.00 for one book, $.25 for each additional. Do not exceed $3.50.

BOOK TOTAL $_____

SHIPPING & HANDLING $_____

APPLICABLE SALES TAX $_____
(CA, NJ, NY, PA)

TOTAL AMOUNT DUE $_____

PAYABLE IN US FUNDS.
(No cash orders accepted.)

SONS OF TEXAS

Book one in the exciting new saga of America's Lone Star state!

TOM EARLY

Texas, 1816. A golden land of opportunity for anyone who dared to stake a claim in its destiny...and its dangers...

Filled with action, adventure, drama and romance, *Sons of Texas* is the magnificent epic story of America in the making...the people, places, and passions that made our country great.

Look for each new book in the series!

B A Berkley paperback on sale in April